Richard Glover

Lyra Piscatoria

Original Lyrics on Fish, Flies, Fishing and Fishermen, Including Poems...

Richard Glover

Lyra Piscatoria
Original Lyrics on Fish, Flies, Fishing and Fishermen, Including Poems...

ISBN/EAN: 9783744782326

Printed in Europe, USA, Canada, Australia, Japan

Cover: Foto ©Andreas Hilbeck / pixelio.de

More available books at **www.hansebooks.com**

LYRA PISCATORIA.

ORIGINAL LYRICS

ON

FISH, FLIES, FISHING AND FISHERMEN,
INCLUDING POEMS ON ALL THE
BRITISH FRESHWATER FISH.

BY

COTSWOLD ISYS, M.A.,

AUTHOR OF

" AN ANGLER'S STRANGE EXPERIENCES," "HANDY GUIDE TO
DRY FLY-FISHING," &c.

Honorary Member of the Fly-Fishers' Club.

LONDON:

HORACE COX,

WINDSOR HOUSE, BREAM'S BUILDINGS, E.C

—

1895.

LONDON:

PRINTED BY HORACE COX, WINDSOR HOUSE, BREAM'S BUILDINGS, E.C.

PREFACE.

Since there is hardly a British fish or a riverside fly of importance, or a phase of angling that is not pourtrayed in these lyrics, the author hopes that they will prove to be welcome to that yearly increasing fraternity, his brother anglers. Criticism on such a book should possess two qualifications; first, a taste for poetry, and secondly, a practical knowledge of each branch of angling. Even those who possess the former may be over-severe on the singer if they are destitute of the latter. For example, their taste may possibly be offended by some of the poems viewed simply æsthetically, such as those on the Eel and the Chub; whereas an angler might see in them a fidelity of description and points about the peculiar character-istics and habits of those fish and their mode of capture, that, so treated, he would keenly appreciate, and feel, moreover, that the very metre and style of those poems were much more artistically appropriate than a metre and style which, by their greater elegance,

would be quite incongruous.   O, æsthetic critic, do
fancy such a thing as being sublime upon an eel, or
pathetic over a chub!

On the other hand, the angler without a taste for
poetry may fail to perceive those touches of imagination that lend a glory to his art, and may mistake for
sentiment what may really be a beautiful attribute of
his recreation, and one which is calculated to add a
pleasure to it that his eyes may never have been
opened to see.

I think these observations will be felt to be just,
and will not be construed by candour into a mere
apology for faults.   The author is not vain enough to
suppose that his work is free from real ones.   He is
only naturally anxious, from the unique peculiarity of
such a book of poems, to bespeak consideration for
some that may, after all, be more apparent than real.
The author's aim has been to ennoble the art he loves,
to refine the taste of anglers, and to intensify and
enlarge their pleasures, by opening up those many
hidden sources of delight that Observation and
Imagination may evoke in the practice of their
charming recreation.   How far he has succeeded
such critics as are possessed of the above qualifications must judge.

SONNET DEDICATORY

TO THE COMMITTEE

AND MEMBERS OF THE FLY-FISHERS' CLUB.

SINCE round my brow unworthy you have placed
The private bay wreath as your Laureate,
'Tis meet that I to you should dedicate
These songs, wherein I tunefully have traced—
A theme the British muse hath never graced—
The portraits of the friends you love so well;
In which, as soft sea music in a shell,
Melodious thoughts and feelings interlaced
By winsome art, play as on Egypt's sands
Round Memnon's statue. Thus would I refine,
As doth the vintner seething must of wine,
The art we love, and seek to glorify
Their pastime who, like you, with pliant wands
Watch the light float or cast the mimic fly.

PROEM.

THE beasts gave ear to Orpheus when he seized
His all-subduing lyre, and to its strains
Sang 'neath the Attic beech his magic song :
But whether man, the nobler beast, would list
Ev'n to the lyre of Orpheus, did the beasts
Form his sole theme—who knows ?
                The Latin bard*
Sang of the beasts and pleased : but gods and men
So mingled with his verse that doubt remains
How far the tuneful Roman would have charmed
The ear of ages, had the beasts alone
Been subject of his song.   But what if *fish*,
So far removed from human sympathies,
So cold of blood, and of so cold a realm,
Had been his theme ? would even Ovid's song
Have caught or kept the ear ?
             True, he of Greece†
Sang of the scaly brood, and in his day
Was laurell'd for his song.   But who now knows

---

* Ovid.
† Oppian born A.D. 192.   Died 222 A.D.   Agesilaus, his father,
was banished from Anazarbus to Malta, by the Emperor
Severus, and his son, Oppian, voluntarily accompanied him, and

Or Oppian or his song, save those that delve
In mausoleums of the lettered past?
And where might Oppian find Severus now?
How then dare one who is no Oppian,
Presumptuous, touch such theme? they well may ask.
I make reply with him whose swan-like song
Was mocked by fools, " I sing because I must." *
Familiar with the waters that I love,
Of river, brook, or mere, long have I grown
Familiar with the finny tribes that take
Their pastime in them.   Mine with them, I love
To take and share, and they to me a joy
Have been since boyhood.   Wherefore, as the joy
Of poet ever must gush forth in song,
(As must his sorrow by an equal law)
My joy took form like this ; but with what fate
I know not.   This I know, that kindred souls
Will be responsive, howsoever few——
Men that have loved, as I, to brush the dew
From morning meads, and, mid the scent of flowers
Pure as the holy incense of a shrine,
To angle where the brook laughs in the sun,
And sings a song as soothing to the heart
As to the ear.   To these elect, I sing.

there wrote among other poems his " Halieutics " in five books.   It
so pleased Severus that he bade Oppian ask what he would and it
should not be denied him.   Oppian piously asked for the restora-
tion of his father to his liberty and country.   Severus not only
granted his request, but presented him with a stater of gold
for each verse, equal to about £5,000 of our money.
    * Tennyson.   In Memoriam, xxi.

Nor shall I lack their audience " fit though few."
Yet it may be that some who angle not
But take delight in all the works of God,
Wherever found, in water, sky, or land,
Admiring all His various handiwork,
May lend me ear, and so perchance may find
That song may please on such unwonted theme.
Thus much by way of prelude would I speak
To Candour : not a word to Charity.
I ask no favour, but I waft my song
Wide to the general ear. If it should please,
Let the musician have his meed ; a boon
Too oft denied in this hard world to those
Who seek to please. However, let it be ;
My secret singing hath its own reward
In but the singing. Should men find a joy
But for a passing moment in the song,
So shall my joy be doubled. Go, then, forth
My songlets on your cold adventurous way !
Having a fear, but cherishing a hope,
I ask no critic to be kind—but just.
Thus Hope lies trembling on these opening leaves
Like some frail thing a breath may blow away,
As sparkles sunlit on the unfolded rose
The liquid diamond of the morning dew.

A few of the poems in the latter part of the volume were published in my former work, "An Angler's Strange Experiences."

CONTENTS.

PART II.—FLIES.

PART III.—FISHING.

PART IV. —FISHERMEN.

PART I.

FISH.

LYRA PISCATORIA.

THE SALMON.

SHAFT of living silver, chased
  With Nature's line of beauty ;
Strength with agile lightness graced,
  Like Love when linked with Duty ;
Glistening with a rainbow sheen
  When the sunray tender
Lights thy scales of pearly green
  With a gleaming splendour.

Native of pure, inland streams,
  Why an ocean lover
Thou becom'st in early dreams,
  Who shall e'er discover ?
Why, when grown to grilse, of sea
  Thou so soon art sated,
And returnest—only He
  Knows who thee created !

Who hath given thee power to know
 Thine own native river,
From all streams that downward flow
 Into ocean ever?
Instinct is a name; no more,
 Not the potence causing;
Let the faithless *that* explore;
 I adore while pausing.

Oh, when home, sweet home's thy song,
 From the sea returning,
With maternal instinct strong
 In thy bosom burning,
What can check thine arrowy course?
 Neither fall nor boulder,
Curving with an innate force
 O'er each barrier's shoulder.

But, O swimmer strong ! beware,
 Resting on thy journey,
Seeking sweet, delicious fare,
 Him who seeks a tourney !
'Ware thee, lest he should deceive
 E'en thine eye sagacious,
Making thee a lie believe
 With a fly fallacious !

Fly to please thy varying mood,*
 Suiting sky and water,

---

* See also " The Salmon Fly," page 69.

Robed in colours many-hued,
    Like a sultan's daughter !
Or, together blended, show
    Like a young moon crescent,
Rising o'er the sunset glow,
    Softly opalescent.

Ah, beware lest thou espy
    The Castle-Connell bending !
Feel that strange, mysterious fly
    With thy strength contending !
Taste it not, it means thee harm !
    Tail it hath— O fear it !—
Link'd with yonder stalwart arm,
    And the gaff is near it !

Oh, thy terror when his barb
    Shall thy fears awaken,
And that fly in gaudy garb
    Cannot be outshaken !
Rush, and leap, and dive ! ah me !
    Vain thy mad endeavour !
No more river, lake, or sea
    Home of thine for ever !

THE TROUT.

CURVED like an Indian bow,
  Bow and arrow in one,
Spotted with crimson, with gold aglow,
  And bright as a summer sun,
With fins like a lady's fan,
  Yet strong as a canvas sail,
Cleaving the stream as a cutter can
  The sea in a Biscay gale.

Like a boat to an anchor fast,
  Thou'rt pois'd by a power within,
Yet swift as lightning thou flashest past,
  By a flap of thy potent fin,
If my rod shall catch thine eye
  Or my cast shall show its sheen :
A water-fox in thy subtlety ;
  Thy sight as an eagle's keen.

Thou lovest the crystal streams
  Where the flowering cresses blow,
Or the freshets dancing in sunny gleams,
  O'er gravelly pebbles flow ;

And even in lazier hours.
  Thou scornest an earthy screen,
But couchest beneath the bank's wild flowers,
  Or the stream-weeds, waving green.

How I love to see thee lie
  In the green, clear watery lane,
In wait for the dainty, floating fly
  Thou hopest so soon to gain!
I would that it might be mine,
  But how hard to make it sail
Adown in that straight, unwavering line
  That shall make deceit prevail!

How hard to suit thy whim,
  So varying with the hour,
Fancying *this* when the day is dim,
  And *that* in shine or shower!
If " out of season " my fly,
  Thou daintiest epicure,
Tho' plied with skill, thy critic eye
  Will scornfully abjure.

A cunning like thine I need
  When I seek to make thee mine :
I must overmatch thee in greed
  In order to conquer thine :

I must study and watch thy ways
    As thou dost mine, with zeal,
Thou valiant foe— I yield thee praise,
    Foe worthy of my steel !

I strike, and the barb is fast !
    The battle has now begun !
We wrestle together at last,
    But the battle is not yet won !
No lover that conquers the fair
    Who long has seemed cold and coy,
Is prouder than I when I draw with a hair
    Thy form to my feet with joy !

THE CHAR.

ENGLAND ! transalpine lakes I know
  And shores where vine and lemon bloom ;
Have angled on the streams that flow
  From Monte Rosa's icy womb ;
Yet never to these whitening years
Have I beheld thy classic meres :

Those lakes where oft in storm and shine,
  Pure Wordsworth piped his pastoral reed ;
Where Coleridge nursed his powers divine,
  And Southey earned a Laureate's meed ;
Where Ruskin 'mid their loved repose
Still weaves his grand, poetic prose.

I dare aver, tho' cynics sneer,
  To me, their hills are mounts of God ;
Those streams are ever doubly dear
  Whose banks the poets' feet have trod ;
But mine a stranger's benison
To Windermere and Coniston.

For Goldsmith's sake, the Temple lanes
  Are memory's gardens fresh and fair;
Bolt Court a golden glory gains,
  Since Johnson wrote and suffered there;
And lovelier lovely scenes appear
For genius sake—like Windermere.

Far grander now the lakeland hills,
  Its valleys wear a brighter green,
More golden are the daffodils,
  And sweeter blows the celandine,
Since Wordsworth's raptured eye gazed on
Winandermere and Coniston.

Fit home to nurse the various muse,
  Where Skiddaw frowns and Rydal smiles,
Where fall on flowers the softest dews,
  And torrents roar thro' wild defiles;
Yet have I known nor joy nor fear
By Coniston or Windermere.

And thus it is, O mystic char!
  I never yet have seen thy face,*
Nor know or whether trout or parr
  Thou art, or child of trout and dace;
Thy pictured form is fair to see,
Tho' doubt doth cloud thine ancestry.

---

* Since this was written, I have had that pleasure, and have
caught char, but on a Scotch loch, and not in "the Lakes."

Thou seem'st like many a maid I've seen
  Within the Foundling's sheltering walls,
Of beauteous form and modest mien,
  On whose fair face the shadow falls,
Since, guiltless of her parent's blame,
She wears for aye the brand of shame.

THE GRAYLING.

O LADY of the river ! drest
    In dainty, silver grey brocade
Which opens o'er thy pearly breast,
    And softens into stripes of shade,
Harmonious as the gentle hues
    Which streak the blossoms of the May,
And grace, o'er grace of form, diffuse,
    As o'er a bride, a bride's array.

What gay coquette, for ball bedight,
    Hath comb of rich-dyed tortoiseshell,
That can, when seen against the light,
    Thy dorsal fin for bloom excel?
Or show a pearl on bosom fair,
    So variegate with rainbow sheen,
As can with that for glow compare
    Which on thy scented robe is seen?*

  * The grayling's skin emits a thymy odour.

Thy tastes become a lady fair,
Thou lov'st the pure and crystal stream
Whose waters ripple brightly where
Old ivied fanes reflected gleam,
And in clear depths, inverted show
The bank-flowers where the bee doth feed,
Or 'neath whose currents lushly grow
The tender greens of waving weed.

No native of our heathen streams,
With holy men thou cam'st at last,
(Or are such legends idle dreams?)
To furnish feast for Friday fast;
In holy water dost thou dwell,
Nigh sacred ruins grey with time,
As listening for the matin bell,
Or music of the vesper chime.*

Coy as a maid, who would thee woo
Must gentle be, nor overbold;
Nor rashly make too much ado
Who would thy dainty form enfold;
Thy timid fears he must allay
And humour well thine every whim ;
If rough or rude, thou skim'st away,
Nor e'er wilt yield thy charms to him.

* It is said that the grayling is not a native of British waters (in only a few of which it is found), but was introduced by the monks for the purpose indicated ; and it is a singular fact that it is found chiefly, if not only, in those streams on the banks of which are the ruins of ancient monasteries.

How often by the sylvan Dee*
    Beside thee I have loved to stand!
And past romantic tower and tree
    To lead thee by a lover's hand
In Haddon's meads, while murmuring Wye
    Has trill'd some sympathetic strain,
In music dear to memory
    I hope with thee to hear again.

        * The Dee in Merionethshire.

THE PERCH.

O GALLANT striped with streamers gay
   Like armour-plated ship of war
At anchor in some sunny bay,
   And bristling o'er with mast and spar !
Thou'rt swift, like her, to chase a foe,
   As prompt as she to seize a prize,
If one or far or near should show
   Its presence to thine argus eyes.

With changing fancy, now I see
   The zebra of the watery plains,
As savage and as wild as he
   Who scours the champaign Nilus drains ;
As fat and sleek with stripèd hide,
   And bristling with as stiff a mane,
Erect with anger and with pride,
   And swelling with a like disdain.

Or yet again let fancy rove,
   And seek thy likeness otherwhere ;
And now an alderman who throve
   And gained with pride the civic chair,

I see, arrayed in robes of state,
  With rounded paunch and ruddy nose,
Suggesting turtle by his gait,
  And pudding by his very hose.

THE DACE.

Swallow of the stream art thou,
  Sporting after summer flies,
Winged with fins that shoot thy prow
  Like a dart towards thy prize.

Swallow-like, thou lov'st the sun,
  Quickened by his potent ray :
Dull thou art when skies are dun,
  Sad thyself, if sad the day.

Sudden as a lightning flash,
  Rising to me ; I must strike
Sudden as thy daring dash ;
  Fish and fisher quick alike.

Loving calm, should sudden breeze
  Ruffle o'er thy glassy roof,
Fear'st thou then the fly to seize,
  Caution then thy sure behoof.

But, beware the angler's art,
  Drop he may beside thy lair,
Bait that can allure thy heart,
  Bait of cunning, seeming fair !

Artful beauty ! to his creel
   Should'st thou by his skill be brought.
Shame of self he need not feel,
   Equal battle has been fought.

THE ROACH.

Thou pride of the Trent, and first gem of the Lea ;
The verse should be gentle that singeth of thee ;
It should glide, like thyself, with a soft easy motion,
As flexile and free as a wave of the ocean.

Like a rose-leaf thy fins, and thy scales like the pearl,
Thou'rt dowered with beauty, arrayed like an earl ;
When fresh from the stream, on the grass thou dost lie
Thy manifold grace is a feast for the eye.

No anchorite thou, and no celibate grim ;
Domestic and true to thy favourite swim :
With thy spouse and thy children thou lovest to roam,
But never too far from the pleasures of home.

Beloved of the toiler who hastens to leave
The city, box-laden, at fall of sweet eve,
To his rivals to prove, in thy capture, his powers ;
Thou symbol to him of his peacefullest hours !

His rod, light and long stretching far o'er the river,
He steadily holds without motion or quiver :
On his crimson-tipped quill as it gently floats by,
Like a hawk on his quarry, he fastens his eye.

See! it trembles! it sinks! with a twitch of his hand,
He has fastened his barb! in a moment his wand
From the butt is disparted! as quickly out flies
To his well-practised fingers the glittering prize!

O, Providence kindly, Who made thee abound
In waters that flow where the toiler is found,
Who, hopeless of pleasures the richer can find,
With thee may find pastime as sweet to his mind!

THE RUDD.

THY name is only fit for prose,
But since thou'rt dowered as the rose,
    I will not fling thee
Aside, offended at thy name,
For thou may'st justly mention claim,
    So I will sing thee.

Nor doth thy name alone offend,
Thy nature is of doubtful blend,*
    And casts a glooming
Shade on thy fame ; yet thou art fair
As rose exotic rich and rare
    In garden blooming.

So have I seen some lovely maid
On whose descent there rests a shade,
    Perforce compelling
That selfless admiration true,
The eye must yield as beauty's due
    Where'er her dwelling.

---

* The Rudd is considered by some naturalists to be a cross
between the roach and the carp.

The more if beauty wedded be
With moral worth of high degree.
            O shame to blight
Her name for fault of parentage !
Rather should wisdom merit gauge
            From depth to height.

Instrinsic worth we all should prize,
No matter where it had its rise,
            Or high or lowly;
Ask not its pedigree, but this—
Is it itself corrupt, or is
            It pure and holy ?

If it itself claim homage, yield
That homage to it; nor conceal'd
            Be courteous bow;
Though others pass it, scornful, by,
Regarding but its ancestry,
            So do not thou !

THE CARP.

Plump and lazy, portly burgher of the fishes! when
    I ask
Fancy's aid in framing numbers in this unpoetic
    task,
Thou the burden of my singing, oh, her look of sad
    despair
Blent with pity for the poet who such task would
    rashly dare!

Pity conquers, and she bids me think of some stout
    Flemish boor
Lolling idly in the sun and drowsing at the tavern
    door ;
Or some warder clad in armour, snoring by a donjon
    keep,
With one eye awake for watching, and the other
    droop'd in sleep.

" Ah, he needs be wary," saith she, "who would pass
    that warder by,
And escape the practised vision of that one sufficient
    eye !

For the shade of shadow creeping would arouse him
    though he saw
Nothing more, and make him wildly forward rush
    and dagger draw."

Aid me, pitying Fancy, further! wave thy wand! ah,
    now I see
German fathers, mothers, children, gathered round
    the Christmas-tree,
What the feast*? my subject knows it; could he
    speak would weeping tell
How, to furnish it, his kindred to their captors fighting
    fell.

Fell, but hardly were they conquered; lusty, strong in
    deadliest strife,
Under heaviest blows of battle, hardly would they
    yield their life;
While the veterans still surviving tooth of time and
    raid of foe,
Hardly will succumb when Nature bids them yield to
    mortal blow.†

---

* Baked carp pie is to the Germans on Christmas Day what
roast beef and plum pudding are to Englishmen.

† The carp is perhaps more difficult to kill than any other fish,
and is remarkable for tenacity of life and longevity. "Buffon
speaks of carp in the fosse of Portchartrain, which were one
hundred and fifty years old, and still possessed all the vivacity and
agility of ordinary fish. Others are spoken of by some authors
which had attained the age of two hundred years."—ROBERT
BLAKEY.

Type, so far, of him who shunneth all the ways of
  wild excess;
Lord of self in youth and manhood, calm in trouble's
  direst stress,
Temperate, pure, and ever loyal to a heavenly
  Master's will,
Hardly him can age enfeeble; hardly him can
  Nature kill!

THE PIKE.

Thou fox of the river, sly, cunning and keen!
Thou savage, finn'd tiger of jungles serene
That, blossoming over with lilies so fair,
Screen thy crocodile eyes in thy watery lair!

O beware! O beware, of those seeming shut eyes
And that long, stealthy form that so motionless lies,
Ye gay finny tribes! ye may deem it indeed
But a log of grey wood that is fixed in the weed.

Yet beware! for that log is all instinct with life:
With murderous passions how savagely rife!
Ah, like a torpedo in war on the sea,
It darts like an an arrow! Oh, hasten and flee!

Too late, for the prize he has marked in the shoal!
See, 'tis borne in his jaws to yon watery goal!
Where long, like Grimalkin, with eyes flashing fire,
He'll play with his victim in joyance of ire.

O *Lucius esox!* beware of the day
When Nemesis comes in an angler's array!
He, too, can be cunning! beware, like Lochiel,
Of his arm which shall strike with the conquering steel!

Ah, by stratagem now he hath lured thee to dart
On the prize that he spins with the cunning of art!
When, lo! as thou gloatest o'er victim thus won,
It strikes like a cobra —and thou art undone!

Like St. Anthon, I call on the fishes to raise
O'er the brave, doughty deed, their loud pæans of
    praise!
And ye anglers! rejoice o'er this cannibal slain,
Rejoice as ye would at the capture of Cain!

THE BREAM.

Of other fish, I've often sought
    To find on land the fellows,
But what thereon is like to thee,
    Except it be a bellows?
Thou flat, big-bellied, slimy thing,
    That lov'st in waters greasy
To bore and wallow in the mud
    Till thou art fat and wheezy.

Oh, why did Nature whose great laws
    Are, for the most, benefic,
Make thee of all fresh-water fish
    By far the most prolific?
Was it to make for other fish
    Some Strasburgh-like confection?
Or did she show in making thee,
    Abnormal imperfection?

Thy slimy skin to touch, to take
    The hook from out thy gills,
To me doth spoil all sport with thee,
    And all its pleasure kills;

I shrink from it as Pat from touch
    Of Acheronian " damon,"
And feel as when against me reels
    Some reeking, drunken drayman.

Yet, sly and shy ! there are who love,
    To overcome thy cunning ;
I leave to them the conqueror's joy,
    Thy scaly foulness shunning ;
They're welcome to the bliss they feel
    Who are to catch thee able ;
Whate'er thy virtues on the rod
    Thou'rt odious on the table.

THE CHUB.

O PITY me, poets, with theme such as this!
'Twould puzzle a Browning or Swinburne, I wis;
Make the bard of L'Allegro grow pensive with care,
And drive Campbell's "Pleasures of Hope" to despair;
Would cool like lime-water the ardour of Burns,
Make Tennyson vainly puff pounds of "returns";
For 'twere easier to spin out "The Tale of a Tub"
Than for poet to grapple the tale of a chub!

But, bound at all hazards the task to essay,
In medias res I must plunge, and pourtray,
If I can, such a likeness that viewers may see,
O chub! one that speaks, or that singeth, of thee.
Imagine a bream dash'd with roach and with dace,
With a little bull's head and a pugilist's face!
Or a fishy bull-terrier, while only a cub,
Would furnish a *carte de visite* for a chub.

And now for thy habitat: How shall I show
The angler who seeketh thee whither to go?
Go then, brother fisher, to streams slow and clear
Which widen to pond, or to lake, or to mere;

Where the green alder droops, or the wavy flag-weed
Shakes down grub or insect on which he may feed:
Near them, or, if warm, lying under a shrub,
If you cautiously peep, you'll discover a chub.

Do you ask, how to take him? "Ah! catch me who
    can!"
Is the taunt he seems ever addressing to man.
Tho' cautious and shy, he's no epicure rare,
But delights in a varied and large bill of fare:
He will sink to a worm, and will rise to a fly,
He will tackle a minnow or swallow paste pie;
While a frog or a bee or a wasp or a grub,
If but skilfully plied, will attract Master Chub.

You may whip for him, sink for him, spin, dib, or dub.
But the *how* of the doing it—there is the rub!
You must watch like a fox, and must creep like a cat.
And conceal all your body, and even your hat!
Your bait must fall light as a leaf from the sky.
And as thistle-down cast on the water your fly;
But if, like a bungler the water you drub
Farewell to your chances of catching a chub!

THE TENCH.

O LADY of the lake whereon
    The water lilies blow,
Or oozy deeps bay out the banks
    Of rivers soft and slow!
No gay coquette e'er looked so fair
    Clad in her satin green ;
No nun behind her nunnery walls
    So shy or seldom seen!

No lady finger's ruby gem
    Can match thy glowing eyes;
Thy satin robe of emerald sheen,
    Her vesture far outvies ;
Yet while she loves her grace to show
    And all her charms display,
Thou, shy and modest water nymph,
    Dost shrink from light of day.

The lover who such prize would win
    Must use all amorous art,
And watch beside thy secret bower
    Bearing love's secret smart;

Must try to meet thee unawares
  When thou com'st forth at eve,
And, patient of repulse, with skill
  By love's own guile deceive.

Then should he win, as win he may,
  A prize so hard to gain,
He well, among the gallants all,
  May boast and not be vain——
That he who could so rare and fair
  A treasure win, should be
Renowned among the wooers round
  In all that brave countree.

THE GUDGEON.

To depict thee, the bard must be wary
Choosing verse that is lightsome and airy,
    It should slip, it should slide,
    It should glance, it should glide,
And trip like the feet of a fairy.

Thou lovest such waters as run bright,
Thy colour's like pearl in a dun light;
    So merry and gay
    Thou wilt play all the day
Like a mote in a beam of the sunlight.

Thy fecundity, oh, how astounding!
In almost all rivers abounding;
    At the task I should quake,
    Of thee census to take,
'Twould be to my senses confounding.

Thou'rt a wondrously delicate biter,
And of bunglers an impudent slighter,
    But when nick'd by fine art,
    As away thou dost dart,
A plucky and game little fighter.

To the juvenile angler ambitious
How dear ! tho' he finds thee capricious :
    Spite thy diet of worms,
    Every *gourmet* affirms
Thou art on the table delicious.

Tho' despised by us proud British anglers,
How oft on the Seine do the danglers
    Of lines plainly show,
    As they stand in a row,
O'er what trifles the French can be wranglers !

And when thou art hook'd what a rabble,
With stamping, viva-ing, and babble,
    Rush down to the quays
    And like goslings or geese,
O'er the wondrous achievement will gabble !

The feat of the hero puts rouge on
His cheek, and he cries out—" 'Tis true, *Jean,*
    Since yesterday week
    I have taken two bleak,
And *voila !* I've captured a *goujon !* "

THE BLEAK.

To image thee on land, thou flashing gem,
   I think of humming birds or dragon flies
That dart, like gleams of light, from stem to stem
   Of sun-kiss'd flowers in their splendrous dyes.

I think of caves beneath " the morning sea,"
   Where laughing mermaids braid their flowing curls,
Where from green rocks the rose anemone
   Rains crimson tints on rounded beads of pearls.*

I think of lambs that frisk round mother ewes
   What time the May is whitening into bloom,
Their downy wool aglist with morning dews,
   Where cowslips shed abroad their sweet perfume.

I think of children over-full of play
   Chasing each other in their wanton joy,
Leaping and skipping thro' the summer day,
   Whom pastime tires not, whom no pleasures cloy.

---

* The scales of the bleak are largely used in the manufacture
of artificial pearls.

I think of many a form of sweet, young life.
  Pure, guileless, tender, undefiled with sin,
The kitten's gambols, and the chicken's strife,
  In playful battle with no hate within.

And as I see thee leaping in the sun,
  So glad, so gay, from care and sorrow free,
Some blessing from the sight my heart has won ;
  Renewal of young life comes into me.

MINNOWS.

Street-boys of the stream, full of frolic,
  Who love on the shallows to play,
And, tho' compassed by foes, melancholic
  Are never, but merry and gay,
Playing hop, skip and jump with each other,
  Hide and seek, and now chasing the flies
Big or little, or fighting a brother,
  And happy in making dirt pies.

Should I, like a "peeler," come near ye,
  Surprised in the midst of your fun,
Like scattering sparrows appear ye,
  When bangs the report of a gun.
Of my size, ye are impudent scorners,
  For my truncheon ye care not a jot,
And, scudding round watery corners,
  Together ye're off like a shot!

But, as bad boys enticed around fiddlers,
  By "peelers" are "spotted" and "nail'd,"
So, often, are cunningest "tiddlers"
  By little boys potted and pail'd;

So beware, lest, in spite of your cunning,
  Some chit, with a pin and a worm,
Should put a full stop to your funning,
  And the worth of my warning confirm !

THE EEL.

EVERY word that doth twist round the tongue, such as
   twirl,
Or hiss thro' the teeth, such as *swivel* or *swirl*,
Or slip o'er them softly, like *slimy* or *slide*,
Or squirm, like a corkscrew, the palate inside,
Or curl up in knots on the tongue like a snake—
Such I need if an eel for a poem I take.
Such words for a poet! O Muses, ye feel
How hapless the bard who must sing of an eel!

They must elongate too (Oh, say not, There's a pun;
For the task I have here is too serious for fun!)
Like elaboration, electricity,
Or, better than either, elliptically.
But I cannot thus linger on strife about words,
I must sing as I can, as in winter the birds,
And my heart 'gainst my fate, like a stoic must steel,
Nor vainly lament that my theme is an eel.

Where shall I begin? at his head or his tail?
They are both much alike, like a sheet and a sail:
His tail often is where his head ought to be,
Like the foot of a rogue in a halter, you see.

He is found in pure water, like whisky, and comes
Too oft, like the drunkard, to sinks and to slums :
He can dart like a spear ; he can turn like a wheel,
For a water street-Arab's this slippery eel.

Elastic as rubber, he'll swallow a rat,
And elope with a duck or a young tabby cat ;
Elusive by nature, your arts he'll elude,
Unless you are artful to study his mood ;
From your hook he will often most cunningly writhe,
And slip thro' the grass with the sound of a scythe,
Unless on a needle you thread a poor worm,
And hold him and your cruelty equally firm.*

Would you have me the art of good dining declare,
And elucidate for you a choice bill of fare ?
Then whene'er to your fancy a *garçon* appeals
And elicits your order, elect fry of eels !
When each luscious morsel you eliminate
From your platter, believe me, you'll feel so elate
That you'll cry, "Oh, Elysium, such dainty reveals,
A feast for a king is a dish of fried eels !

---

* This barbaric mode of baiting a worm on a needle is vulgarly
called "sniggling," and is much practised by a certain class of
anglers on the river Lea.

THE BARBEL.

Thou bearded water-hog, with thee
　　Must song its page defile ?
O theme a bard would gladly shun
　　Who hateth all things vile !
But since a Burns sang mouse and louse,*
　　Nor rats made Browning shiver,†
I'll sing thee, Falstaff of the stream,
　　And Blue Beard of the river.

Thou'rt good for nought, like Zola's page ;
　　E'en sport with thee is foul ;
Who feeds on thee is carrion-fed,
　　Unclean, as bat or owl ;
I envy not his vulgar taste
　　Who but to catch thee wishes ;
Thy touch alone defiles the hand,
　　Thou Paul de Koch of fishes !

---

* *Vide,* "To a Louse on a Lady's Bonnet," and "To a Mouse,"
by Robert Burns.
† *Vide,* "The Pied Piper of Hamelin," by Robert Browning.

Thy grovelling form doth never rise,
Thou hatest all things pure ;
So never insect of the air
Can thy gross eye allure,
Nor dainty fish of silver streams,
Nor pastel unpolluted ;
Alone the maggot, worm and slug
Are to thy palate suited.

Thou hatest light the sun by day,
And moon and star by night ;
Thy joy is with the water-ghouls,
And garbage thy delight ;
The water-witches croon with thee,
And wanton with thy wattles,
In caverns strown with filthy slime
And rags and broken bottles.

In fish I find the types of men,
But can man fall so low
To bear a likeness unto thee ?
Ah, Truth ! wilt thou say, No ?
O would thou could'st with show of proof
Denounce it as a libel !
But Charity herself is check'd
By witness of thy Bible.

She hears thee speak of those who love
　　Gross darkness more than light;*
Who eat up sin as Sodom ate,
　　With hungry appetite;†
Who, like fed horses in the morn,
　　Neigh after what is evil,‡
And hate the holy, pure and good,
　　As doth their sire the Devil.§

And is her witness true or false?
　　Cast pearls to human swine—
The pearls of heaven—and see how far
　　Their tastes to them incline!
But oh! behold the magnet force
　　Of hooks with evil baited!
And see in every land the crowds
　　With wine and whoredom sated!

See if no barbel antitypes
　　Delight in —da's page!
If none applaud in pit or box
　　The Anglo-Gallic stage!
Who loves them, or from Ratcliff slum,
　　Or western halls of marble,
Doth by the act declare himself
　　A literary barbel.

---

* John iii. 19, 20.　　† Hosea iv. 8.　Isa. iii. 9.
‡ Jer. v. 8.　　§ John viii. 44.

Ask of our Magdalen asiles,
  Who fill them with their prey?
In gambling hells and dens of lust,
  Who lead pure youth astray?
And when ye look for trees that bear
  These fruits of Adam's apple,
Be sure ye scan Belgravian squares
  As well as low Whitechapel!

A ROUNDELAY OF THE FISHES.

Hand in hand, or fin by fin,
Let us now our song begin,
Fish that in fresh waters play,
Sing ye all a roundelay!

Salmon, noble lord and king,
Lead us in the song we sing!
Join him grayling, trout and char,
With his children grilse and parr!

Join ye gudgeon, bleak and dace,
And ye fish of meaner race,
Roach and carp of pond or stream,
Perch and pike and eel and bream!

Barbel huge, and minnow small,
Tench and rudd, come one and all.
All together sing to-day
Glad and grateful roundelay!

Let us to the bard of fish
Offer every loving wish!
Flap we all our fins in glee
That at length a bard have we!

SUPPLEMENTARY :

THE CRITIC ANTICIPATED.

JUDICIOUS readers all will feel
  My list is long enough,
Altho' I've neither said nor sung
  One word about *the Ruff.*

Judicial critics, ne'ertheless,
  Will say, " What poor invention
Our bard has, since *the Lamprey* finds
  Within his book no mention.

Indeed, to be a guide complete
  His book makes no approach ;
Suffice to say he passes o'er
  That British fish *the Loach !*

And, not to mention other faults,
  We wonder why he's mute
About that fish " (they'll prove it fish !)
  " To wit, the British *Newt.*

Nor can we find from first to last—
  We think a fatal lack---
Ode, song, or sonnet, not a line
  About *the Stickleback ! "*

Perhaps, indeed, that *is* a fault,
　And did I better know 'em,
I do confess that sticklebacks
　Might well deserve a poem.

Not Wren himself, nor Gilbert Scott,
　Their skill in architecture
Could overpass, I heard affirmed
　In Wood's delightful lecture.*

And, when in love, they change their hues
　In such a wondrous fashion,
As might an opal, could it feel
　The flame of amorous passion.

And, when they're crossed in love, I hear,
　They so stick up their backs—
From whence their name—that rivals all
　Fly, fearful of their whacks.

While, as to matrimonial ways,
　They're full of love and wonder,
And preach a lesson *they* might learn
　Whom Jeune doth put asunder !†

Thus ev'n the humble stickleback,
　Right home this moral brings,
That poetry and mystery
　Surround the meanest things.

* The late Rev. J. G. Wood, M.A., naturalist and lecturer.
† Sir Francis Jeune, Judge in the Divorce Court.

PART II.

FLIES.

THE FEBRUARY RED.

Thou living bud that wingest
  From winter's frozen palm,
With unborn summer tinted,
  Thy breath her unfelt balm;
When I see thee on the brooklet,
  I hear the snowdrops ring,
And ere I hear the cuckoo
  Thou singest of the Spring!

Thou art the insect cuckoo,
  Come sooner than the bird,
To whisper soft her prophecy
  That soon there will be heard
The turtle's voice in all the land
  And singing birds to cheer
Our ears and hearts with those pure notes
  The angels love to hear.

Thou art the scout of Summer,
  Sent forward on her war
With Winter, to spy out the land,
  And herald her from far;

To say, her fiery legions
    Shall follow in thy train
And plant bright flags of victory
    Above his cold domain !

Thou art a John the Baptist
    Come to the riverside,
Clad in a sober garment,
    Yet crying far and wide
Good news that Spring is coming,
    With hope and joy and flowers,
To ripen to full summertide
    With all its rosy hours.

Bloom on the white of Winter !
    Of river-flies first-born ;
Pulse of the primest sap of life,
    Ere green hath tipp'd the thorn !
Before the crocus peepeth
    Above the frozen earth,
Thou sayest, Resurrection-life
    Is coming to the birth !

To me, a wingèd angel,
    To hail a glad New Year
Of angling joys, thou seemest ;—
    An angel that doth cheer

My heart with forward visions
  Of joys by laughing streams,
That now seem near, but O so long
  Have been but winter dreams !

THE MARCH BROWN.

O SOBER-VESTED wingling! why
    Thus seek these waters cold,
While windy sleet drives thro' the sky
    And whistles o'er the wold ?
This fitful sun that lights thy form
    And tempts thee forth to-day,
Can scarce suffice the heart to warm
    That trembles in its ray.

And yet how nobly dost thou brave
    Thy cold and adverse fate,
That this pale gleam above the wave
    Can merely mitigate !
A passing joy that's hardly joy
    Seems all thou hop'st to find ;
No gold of life but much alloy,
    Child of the chill east wind !

'Tis March with many here below
    Almost throughout their life ;
How rarely doth their west-wind blow,
    With east winds e'er at strife !

Misfortune seems to claim them hers,
  And turns to sleet their showers;
Of Hope they are the prisoners,
  The prickly gorse their flowers!

And yet for them some primrose blows,
  And hidden violets bloom;
To give them joy some streamlet flows;
  No life is *only* gloom!
Their roughest month hath some soft days,
  Some antepasts of May,
To whisper hope and lift to praise
  And make the saddest gay.

Nor breathes there one who may not have
  A hope when life is done
(All thanks to Him who came to save
  This sad world's saddest son!)
Of putting off this sombre vest,
  Bedropp'd with tears, may be,
And putting on in realms of rest
  Joy's immortality.

THE ALDER.

Æsop taught us—nay, each poet
    Ever brings the truth to mind,
Did not observation show it,
That all grades of lower being
        Image forth mankind.

Hence my fancy often traces,
    Even in ephemeræ,
Human masks and human faces
Like to those that meet my vision
        In society.

Even insects make me merry,
    And, not seldom, sad withal ;
Now they make me laugh ; then very
Grave with thoughts that make me sagely
        Philosophical.

When the Mayfly bursts in beauty
    From the stream and flutters down,
Seeking pleasure, scorning duty,
There I see the girl of fashion
        " Coming out " in town.

When I see, some moments after,
  Lurking trout cut short her bliss ;
Ah ! what neighbours tears and laughter,
Joy and sorrow, life and death are
      In a world like this.

When a graceful, light and airy
  Red-quill danceth down the stream,
Robed in gauze, a sparkling fairy,
Like Titania, then I dream a
      Midsummer-Night's Dream.

Comes a dragoness-fly sailing
  Towards some aphis paly-green !
Ah ! I feel for it a quailing,
As I feel for Duncan, seeing
      Macbeth's bloody queen !

Now a bumble-bee falls over,
  Rolling like a drunken lord,
From a bending stalk of clover,
Fat as Falstaff, till I laugh like
      Mistress Page or Ford.

Then an olive-dun comes winging
  On the zephyr, like a queen
Of some airy realm, and bringing
Up to fancy pure and graceful
      Maids like Imogene.

Then, while on the grass reclining,
　　Thou com'st by in cloak of brown,
Dear old maid ! and 'neath its lining,
I can fancy bounteous basket
　　　　Borne to neighbour town.

Borne to cheer some sick friend lying
　　There in pain, in need of thee,
Aye, it may be near to dying,
For thy back is bent in sorrow,
　　　　Toddling wearily.

Type of many an olden maiden,
　　Fashion scorns with eye askant,
Who to hundreds sorrow laden,
Tho' so plain and humble, yet are
　　　　Angels ministrant.

List, O critic ! mine a pride ill
　　Suited to an honest bard,
Should I claim that charming idyll
As mine own, another higher
　　　　Merits the reward.*

---

* See the famous passage on the Alder in Charles Kingsley's
" Chalk Stream Studies " (Prose Idylls) which suggested the three
previous stanzas.

Envious of thee, humble alder,
　Might, indeed, be many men,
Since thou sharest with a Balder,
Hereward, and Drake, and Raleigh,
　Praise from Kingsley's pen !

THE MAYFLY (*Ephemera Danica*).

A PARABLE.

I TURNED a stone o'er which the brooklet brawl'd,
And from beneath a loathsome creature crawl'd
Half insect and half reptile.   I, appall'd,

Shrank lest the savage, six-legged, wormy thing,
Should seize my heedless hand and on it cling,
And pierce it with some sharp, polluting sting.

" Thou hideous water-devil, hence ! " I cried,
While 'neath a weed it seemed in shame to hide,
And to my ear of fancy, thus replied :—

" Ah, scorn me not, nor judge by what you see ;
Time, that works wonders, may do much for me.
And what I am, I may not always be ! "

I lay me down upon the bank to view
The creeping horror closely, shape and hue,
The warm sun glancing the pure water thro',

When, like Ithuriel's spear, the potent ray
Pierced the foul thing, which rose to air and day,
And, bubbling, burst into a beautous fay.

One moment in the sun she fans her wings
And smooths to roundness all their mazy rings,
Then, native to the summer air she springs.

Beware, O beauty! in the streamlet lies
A gay-robed gallant with adoring eyes;
Meet not his kiss, for she he kisseth dies!

So, unbeheld, the antique Satyr hath
Gazed thro' the boskage on the dainty path
Of Daphne, trembling to her morning bath.

Rising and falling o'er the waters clear,
She floats away in bliss; and on my ear
Her wise rebuke I seem again to hear—

" Ah, scorn me not, nor judge by what you see;
Time, that works wonders, may do much for me,
And what I am, I may not always be!"

Ah! we misjudge by seemings! what may lie
Hid 'neath the wrappage loathsome to the eye,
He only knows who can the heart descry!

Musing, I went upon my homeward way,
Conning that lesson from the fly of May,
Which never from my heart will pass away.

I hear it in the crowded city when
I meet the drunkard reeling from his den
Or pass the sinful midnight Magdalen.

And still it speaks beside the dying bed,
Where some poor Christian lays his lowly head
In pain and poverty—that voice which said :—

" Ah, scorn me not, nor judge by what you see ;
Time, that works wonders, may do much for me,
And what I am, I may not always be ! "

THE OLIVE DUN.

BEAUTIFUL Venus was born of the sea,
　Near to the Paphian isle ;
Thou, little Olive, as lovely as she,
　Art born of the river's smile,
The river that gladdens this mead so fair
　With music of rippling waters
That play to thy dance in the sunny air,
　Thou fairest of all her daughters !

Venus was born to be loved and love,
　As beauty is wide-world o'er,
Sighing, as for her mate the dove,
　For the mermen of cave and shore ;
And thou, little beauty, with love aglow
　Art now on this ripple sailing
In search of a lover, the stream below,
　To rise to thy charms prevailing.

Ah, little Olive, beneath the stream
　Are they who love but of guile,
Who flatter, admire and basely scheme
　Their ruin on whom they smile !

So beware. lest in seeking a lover true,
　A traitor should mark thy beauty,
And thou shoulds't discover and vainly rue
　How Lust scorns love and duty!

TO THE QUILL GNAT.

Sunshine's blissful, beautiful daughter,
Sailing over the sheeny water,
    Gliding so gleefully gay ;
Tremulous, tiny, gauzy, airy,
Dreamy, downy, delicate fairy,
    Whither, O whither away ?

Wait but awhile on the way that thou wingest ;
Sing me one strain of the song that thou singest !
    Pause on this pendulous spray !
Pause and some pleasure impart
To the sight of my eyes and the love of my heart,
    Then wing if thou wilt, on thy way !

F

THE SONG OF THE RED SPINNERS.

Up and down; in and out;
Now within; now without;
Falling in; falling out;
    Buzzing our glee.
Winging and singing,
And singing and winging,
And winging and singing,
    How happy are we!

Sing away; wing away!
Live to-day; love to-day!
Dance in the dancing ray!
    Sing, never sigh!
Life—O the bliss of it!
Love—O the kiss of it!
Death—We know this of it,
    Dancing we die!

THE COACHMAN.

O, buzzy and fuzzy, dark body of herl,
  With thy pure, white silken wing!
The bard of the rod were indeed a churl
  To refuse of thee to sing,
Who so oft hast driven him home with glee
  When weary with hopeless toil,
In a merry late hour when but for thee
  He had carried no finny spoil.

With thy summer cape and thy woolly vest,
  Prepared for the chill night air,
Like thy mates of town for night work drest,
  To ply for a nightly fare,
Thou comest, the moths about thy head,
  Thy music the beetle's hum,
While the stars wink out of the river bed,
  And the woodland sounds are dumb.

Thou hast oft pulled up on my homeward way,
  And bid me mark a rise,
Hast stealthily gone to the hidden prey
  And landed the golden prize ;

When eve to silvery moonlight wore,
   Thou hast crept to the darkling stream
And gladdened my eyes by added store,
   Till thy prowess seemed a dream.

O, tis hard to carry an empty creel
   At the close of a sultry day,
And, trudging the homeward path, to feel
   All art has been thrown away !
But if so vainly for trout you strive,
   At gloaming never despair,
Call on your coachman to give them a drive,
   And he will not want a fare !

THE SALMON FLY.

"Not an insect that flies in our northern sky,
  Nor a worm that doth crawl on our British soil,
Resembles this thing you denominate ' fly,'
  With its wools and its feathers and golden foil,
And yet it is plain that the salmon will take
  This utter monstrosity fishermen ply.
For *what* do the salmon the wonder mistake?
  For to me 'tis inscrutable mystery."

" A riddle no longer, I think, it will be,
  If you only remember what well you know,
That the salmon I take inhabit the sea,
  Tho' they come to these rivers to spawn their roe;
And deep in the caves of the warm southern seas
  Are sweet, dainty zoophytes, fairily hued,
To salmon the richest of delicacies,
  And *this* they mistake for that exquisite food."

TO THE DRAGON FLY.

FLASHING gem on silver-netted,
   Fan-like, dryly-rustling wings,
Chased with wondrous art, and fretted
   With that curious maze of rings :
On this leaf thy form doth quiver,
   Like an arrow in a targe,
Shot by elfin of the river,
   Sporting viewless on its marge.

Like some glistering, gleaming jewel
   On some beauty's restful hand,
Art thou, yet I feel thee cruel,
   As I o'er thee raptly stand :
Flash ! thou'rt gone ! not wont to linger ;
   'Tis as though from out her ring
Sprang the gem, and from the finger
   Suddenly took wing.

"THE ANGLERS' CURSE."

(MIDGES.)

WHAT means this strange commotion
That makes this pool so like a seething ocean,
 And every fish within it mad with glee,
Rising and sucking down some rare confection
That baffles all my closest introspection,
 For naught upon the water can I see?

Ah, 'tis that imp of evil,
That miniature edition of the devil
 Which, entering the twice a thousand swine,
Made them rush madly down the cliffy height,
And lash Gennesaret's blue to foamy white,
 As now these trout, O Test! lash madly thine!

How such a tiny dainty
Can with such joy of lust, O trout, attaint ye,
 Were past believing were it not so plain ;
Is it because 'tis like the *petit verre*
Of curaçoa or flav'rous olives rare
 The gourmand tastes fresh appetite to gain?

It cannot be for diet,
Since millions hardly could keep hunger quiet,
   Each scarcely larger than a sunbeam's mote;
It must possess some unimagined flavour,
Some sweet ambrosia of elysian savour,
   For epicures of this late *table d'hote.**

" The Angler's Curse " they name it,
But whence the reason why they so defame it ?
   Is it because the angler doth despair
Of other fly to tempt whilst it doth spot
Unseen the water? for, I hope 'tis not
   Because it causes the profane to swear.

Yet if there's ought could tempt me
To passion's speech, or from its guilt exempt me,
   I feel 'tis thou, thou microscopic pest,
That winds the angler's hope to pitch so high,
And every lure he knows in vain to try,
   While winking trout turn all his art to jest.

---

* These midges generally come on most thickly in the midst of the evening rise.

MOTHS.

WHEN eve her glooming shadow throws
  Athwart the meads and o'er the stream,
  The while, heat-weary, day doth dream
Adroop, as doth the folded rose,

Then forth ye come to dance and play
  In velvet robe and sandall'd shoon,
  'Neath light of star and crescent moon,
Lov'd better than the light of day.

Who know your darkling wont are those
  Who love the gloom of mantled night,
  And 'neath its cloak and screen'd from sight
They lurk unseen, your wily foes.

They lie in wait, they watch your ways,
  And seem to love, but only seem ;
  They seek your life, and yet ye dream
They love ye while their eyes speak praise.

Ah, foolish moths ! the starry sheen
  Ye fly to in the glittering wave,
  Is but the spangle o'er the grave ;
The glitter, not the grave, is seen !

Ye lightly laugh, like your compeers,
    Ye hate wise words that give ye pain,
    And him who speaks; and so in vain
The warning bathed in Pity's tears.

I see ye hover o'er the gleam,
    That seems a star, but is a grave :
    A bubble; ah, who now shall save?
Your dream of pleasure is a dream !

Your false adorer's lustful eyes
    Have marked your weakness, to betray ;
    As Guile marks many a maiden gay
Who towards the glare of Folly flies.

PART III.

FISHING.

FISHING.

L'espoir est ma force.

HOPE in my heart, health in the air,
The freshness of morning everywhere,
Pleasure before, and care behind,
I tramp to the river with gleesome mind,
And with brotherly love to all mankind !
And the tramp of my eager feet doth say,
I wonder, I wonder, what luck to-day !

Fear begone ! and away with Doubt !
The river, I know, is full of trout ;
Do ye say " Yon cloud may blacken the sky,
Or weeds may come down, or—pigs may fly ? "
I'm ready for all, and what care I ?
And the tramp of my eager feet doth say,
I wonder, I wonder, what luck to-day !

" Good morning," says one, " I wish you sport ! "
And he brings of the river a good report :

" They were rising like fun when I came by."
And I tramp on my way more cheerfully,
Such power in a hopeful word doth lie !
And the tramp of my feet doth plainly say,
I hope for good luck indeed to-day !

Off the road, and on to the grass,
Two sweet meadows to overpass ;
Beautiful sound that buzzing of flies,
Bringing my heart up into my eyes !
Ha ! what was *that?* a magnificent rise !
Oh ! I hope to-night to my friends to say,
What splendid luck I have had to-day !

Noon : Dinner al fresco.

" Sub tegmine fagi, me, O Tityre,"*
    Behold now enjoying my dinner,
Two chops fried in eggs, and some cool bitter B
    —A repast fit for Alderman Skinner !
While my creel and my rod and my line on the grass
    Lie at rest with my little red-spinner.

---

* A few brother anglers may be glad to have a free translation
of this free Latin : " Behold me, O Tityrus ! under this spreading
beech tree ! "

O Tityre! I believe that this tree
  Is the son of a seedling that Maro
Picked up in Italia, and sent o'er the sea
  To some consul in Britain afar, O !
And this bitter's Falernian, or else I do dream,
  It never came forth from a bar, O !*

Blest beech ! O, how sweet to my eye is thy shade !
  And how restful thy bark to my back, O !
And no carpet that ever in Persia was made,
  Or wove in the looms of Astrakko,
Was so soft as this grass ! Oh, I feel like a Shah,
  Smoking on it my pipe of tobacco !*

O, surely this day's an Arabian Night,
  Or my fancy now taking a tour is ;
Those seeming tall poplars are platans moon-bright,
  And yon turkey apparent, I'm sure, is
A peacock; while those that seem'd haymaking jades,
  Are gauzy-veil'd, exquisite houris !

And what this white incense that silvers the green,
  As though from spice gardens it clomb ? ah !
The artist that could but depicture this scene
  Would be worthy a royal diploma ;
And Phemè should write of his work to the Queen
  On a page that should breathe this aroma !

* See foot-note on page 97.

Homewards: Evening.

The crimson-tinted gloaming fades.
　　The sheeted silver of the stream
Is darkening into sombre shades,
　　And day dies like a happy dream;
And now, my rod, the time is come
　　　　　　For home—sweet home!

The distant sheep-bell faintly rings
　　Above the young lamb's plaintive bleat;
The drowsy bat on shadowy wings
　　Sails round the homestead's snug retreat;
Mute is the wheel of yonder mill—
　　　　　　How calm! how still!

The meadow path is damp with dew,
　　The rooks flap toward their woodland nest,
The gazing kine the sweet cud chew,
　　All nature soothes itself to rest;
What peace, what joy to all is given!
　　　　　　How kind is heaven!

Afar I hear the minster bells
　　Swing faintly out their evening chime,
In soothing falls, and cheering swells,
　　That with my homeward feet keep time,
And gratitude my heart o'erwells,
　　　　　　Dear, holy bells!

SUNDAY.

THREE days of eastern gales; but now so calm!
    And zephyrs, West!
The sun shines warm, shedding a holy balm
    Of soothing rest.

A rise is on that makes the water foam.
    Fish seem to say,
" We unmolested now, may fearless roam,
    'Tis Sabbath day."

Here, near my inn, alone on holiday,
    Temptation cries,
" Come, seize occasion, lest it pass away :
    Take rod and flies!"

But holy duty hears the village bells
    In rise and falls,
Calling to other joys across the dells
    From sacred halls.

G

Temptation at the sound grows pale and flies
　　　Ashamed away ;
And from the stile at once resolved I rise
　　　To praise and pray.

And on the morrow, tho' it prove less fair,
　　　A keener zest
I know I shall enjoy if I go there
　　　For holy rest.

" Nor finding thine own pleasure."* Worship not,
　　　Angler, thy rod !
He ne'er found pleasure who for it forgot
　　　To worship God.

* Isa. lviii. 13.

THE MUSIC OF THE REEL.

SONG FOR THE OPENING OF THE TROUT SEASON.

HAIL ! soft and genial vernal morn !
  Hail! brooklet flowing clear !
O, joy, with rod in hand again
  To greet our opening year !
While Hope's bright pleasures cheer my heart,
  And o'er my fancy steal,
As on my ear so sweetly rings
  The music of the reel !

It sings of winter past and gone,
  Of daily lengthening hours,
When sunny spring shall gaily bring
  The cuckoo and the flowers ;
When oft amid the meads my rod
  Shall lightly wave, and feel
The leaping trout arise and ring
  The music of the reel !

Nor Hope alone is in the tone
  This sweetest music gives,
But many a happy memory wakes,
  Thus started, and re-lives

Of morn and eve by river side,
  And easefull noon-day meal,
While slept upon the resting rod,
  The music of the reel!

But Hope o'er Memory now prevails,
  And fans her forward wing;
And as I lift anew the rod
  I hear her cheerly sing—
May coming days be best of all,
  And fuller fill the creel,
And richer spoil reward thy toil
  With music from the reel!

CAPTAIN TROUT AND THE MAYFLY.

May is come, to trout so dear,
Month of months of all the year!
Warm the water, soft and clear,
Soon the Mayfly will be here!
    Ope your eyes and shake your fins!
    Now the feast of feasts begins!
    For the revels all prepare!
    O the dainties rich and rare!

Ha! up yonder what is *that*,
Winged with beauty, long and fat?
Let me now arise and see
If, indeed, 'tis really he!
    Ope your eyes and shake your fins!
    Now the feast of feasts begins!
    For the revels all prepare!
    O the dainties rich and rare!

No mistake about it, boys!
O that antepast of joys!
'Twas indeed the pioneer!
Swarms for all will now appear!
    Ope your eyes and shake your fins!
    Now the feast of feasts begins!
    For the revels all prepare!
    O the dainties rich and rare!

" Now's the day, and now's the hour ! "
See, the cloudy swarm doth lour!
Now, ye trout, arise and kill,
And of plenty take your fill!
    Ope your eyes and shake your fins!
    Now the feast of feasts begins!
    For the revels all prepare!
    O the dainties rich and rare!

Are ye ready ? upward flash!
Downward, upward, slap and dash!
Thro' the bubbling waters crash,
Splash and dash and flash and clash!
    Ope your eyes and shake your fins!
    Now the feast of feasts begin!
    For the revels all prepare!
    O the dainties rich and rare!

THE ANGLER'S CONCERT.

THERE are who say the angler's sport is dull,
  Who pity him as lonely in the meads;
Not they who know, for earth and heaven are full
  Of sweet companions; and he only needs
Quick eye and ear; then beings beautiful
  Abound to speak and sing to him who heeds.
Hark! hark, " the lark " e'en now " at heaven's gate
    sings,"
And shakes down dropping music from his wings!

He is my morning chorister, and long
  I drink the strains of his delirious joy;
Then greets me soon another friend in song,
  The sudden blackbird with shy glances coy.*
He starts, but knows my rod so lithe and long
  No fowler's gun that need his fears annoy :
Then in the copse alighting, charms my ear
With glad, full-throated music, strong and clear.

* " Sudden." The author has an impression that this epithet
occurs in a similar connection in Keats, but he cannot verify the
quotation.

I pass the lawns, and now his music fades ;
　　I near the ash that dips into the stream,
Gay linnets carol in its leafy shades,
　　O'erfull of gladness in the morning beam,
Then wheeling fly ; and now from those thick glades
　　I catch sweet undertones of softer theme,
Awhile the cooings of full-breasted doves
Ripple the silence with their murmuring loves.

I reach the bridge, and pausing, rest awhile
　　And gaze into the river flowing clear,
And there from off a little stony isle—
　　A lichen-covered boulder—greets my ear
The ouzel's low tweet-tweet ; with many a wile
　　And graceful curtsey, coy and void of fear,
She views me archly ; then with sudden flight
Circles the gnat with sateless appetite.

My creel once more I o'er my shoulders fling,
　　And whip the upward stream for finny spoil ;
And now the kingfisher with lightning wing
　　Flashes before me, while, to cheer my toil,
The warbling thrush doth in the hawthorn sing,
　　Untwisting harmony's most secret coil.
Delights so various thus around me throng
Now charmed with beauty, and now cheered by song.

And when at sultry noon beneath the shade
   Of some umbrageous tree I seek repose,
And song is hush'd in all the neighbouring glade,
   And tired eyes upon the landscape close,
Cool, falling waters from the near cascade,
   Which from some tributary brook o'erflows,
Blend with the buzz of insects in the beam,
And soothe my senses to a sweet day-dream.

Nor need I haste to break its fancy spell,
   For useless is the toil of afternoon
While glows the sun, the fisher knows too well,
   When 'neath the weeds the very fish do swoon;
Nor will they wake until the vesper bell
   Greets eve, apparelled in a crescent moon,
And the declining sun toward the west
Proclaims the angler's hour, the sweetest, best.

Arise! for see the dimpling water tells
   Of finny life astir that stirs my own!
Like Prospero, I whisper magic spells
   To my lithe wand in comprehended tone;
Then music softly sounds, like Ariel's,
   From yonder copse it cometh gently blown
On Zephyr's wing; O, list! the nightingale
With throbbing heart pours forth her lovelorn tale!

Now flush the waters in the afterglow
   That eastward reddens from the crimson west;
Awhile the rooks, with weary wing and slow,
   Flap homeward to their fledglings in their nest,
And on my listening ear, so far below,
   Their cawings sound a lullaby of rest,
Nor harsh the tones, but full of sweet repose ;
Nor fitter music could the concert close.

THE WATER OUZEL.

GAY little lady, thou belle of the river,
  Ever coquetting its smile to obtain,
Oft of its kisses receiver and giver,
  Now giving joy to it, now giving pain :

Joy—by thy beauty and gentle advances ;
  Pain—by thy coyness in flitting away ;
Joy—by the spell of thy maidenly glances ;
  Pain—that they do not more restfully stay.

Where is the maiden or gay belle of fashion,
  Rounded to shape of a slenderer grace ?
Soul hast thou pure as the lilies of passion,
  Form that all harmonies seem to embrace.

Where is the daughter of wealth or of pleasure
  Robed with an elegance matching with thine ?
Which treads the dance with a daintier measure ?
  Moves with a motion of music so fine ?

Watching thy ways is a lesson æsthetic,
  Moulding to taste both the eye and the mind ;
Lessons indeed more divinely pathetic
  Scholar reflective unseeking may find.

Careless thou art of the needs of to-morrow,
  Taking with joy what is given to-day,
Void of the doubt and the fear and the sorrow
  Even our faith cannot wholly allay.

Monitress beautiful, missioned by Heaven,
  Joy at beholding thy grace has been mine,
Yet what rebuke to my heart thou hast given,
  Teaching me trust and contentment like thine !

THE WATER VOLE.

On the flotsam of weed 'neath the bank of the stream,
　Where the lily hath rooted and blooms so white,
While I lie on the sward in a sweet, summer dream,
　Thy soft form creepeth thro' flecks of light.

And I watch thine eye with its timid glance,
　And the lustrous glow of a Persian maid's,
While above thee the leaves of the alder dance
　In a beautiful mingle of lights and shades.

And I see thee poised on thy flowery barge,
　Preening thy face with a sweet content,
And anon swim off to a freshet marge,
　To feed on the cresses with ravishment.

Who feedeth the ravens, provideth for thee,
　And giveth thee joy in thy juicy fare ;
O, fear not a foe in that vision of me !—
　Ah ! gone with a plunge to thy hidden lair !

BROOK MUSIC.

Like the harp of an angel, pure, dulcet, and clear,
　That keeps happy time to the air that he sings,
My brooklet art thou to my fanciful ear;
　Thy streams are his fingers, thy stones are its strings,
And on them for ever, by night and by day,
A music of heaven thou sweetly dost play.

So artless its tones, yet no effort of art
　Can weave such a melody, try as it will;
Alike solemn Haydn and sprightly Mozart
　Would yield thee the palm in despair of their skill;
To soothe as thou soothest, how would they rejoice!
At best they are echoes, but thou art a voice.

There's a " song without words " in thy sweet under-
　　tone
　No speech can embody, nor music define,
Not e'en the sad raptures of sweet Mendelssohn,
　For this is a music that's purely divine!
God's peace thou bring'st down from the heart of the
　　hills,
And like sleep on tired eyes thy nepenthe distils.

As I lie on this bank with thy strain in my ear,
  While the breeze that thou coolest is fanning my
    brow,
I feel that I hardly could fret should I hear
  The voice that of life would unburden me now—
The voice that once bade all the tumult to cease,
Of the storm-troubled sea, and at once there was
  peace !

WEEDS.

If there be above another
One annoyance that doth smother
All my patience, angling brother,
And make me savage with my mother,
       'Tis the weeds.

Down they come in swirls and rushes,
Grass and thistles, thorns and bushes !
All at once the rising hushes,
And my naughty anger flushes—
       Hang the weeds !

O, that unseen wretch above there !
He hath little of my love there,
With his busy hand in glove there ;
Will no friends give him a shove there
       In the weeds ?

Well he seems to know 'tis *my* day ;
Well how he can spoil my high day,
For he always chooses Friday,
Bank and bush to render tidy,
       Cutting weeds !

They unman me, they unmake me;
Now doth Fortitude forsake me !
Fell despair doth grimly shake me—
All its horrors overtake me
Thro' the weeds ?

Passion cannot be defended,
Nor bad luck by wrath be mended,
So I'll not wish him extended,
All his hateful toiling ended,
'Neath the weeds.

What shall soothe my soul's vexation ?
What shall calm my indignation ?
Ha ! I'll seek some consolation—
Oh what fitting compensation!—
In the weed !*

* It does not follow from this (or from " Noon," p. 79) that the author is not a very enthusiastic member of the Anti-Tobacco League ; nor that he is not an ardent disciple of Sir Wilfrid—does it ? Nor is there any proof in " Noon " that the beverage was not Kop's Ale. The poet is a dramatist, " holding the mirror up to " —anglers as they are. Shakespeare was neither Falstaff nor Stephano.

HAMPSHIRE FLY-FISHING.

DRY-FLY.

[These two are exact descriptions of the two totally different
styles.]

ONE, two, three! and the wavy line
    Backward and forward flies,
Four! and there falls, as a gossamer light,
    On the further ring of the rise,
My gay quill-fly, with her wings so dry,
    And she sails on the flowing stream
As a nautilus sails on a summer sea,
    Or a fairy floats in a dream!

True is the cast, and she wings her way
    In a line as straight and true,
Thro' the widening rings, as the famous "line"
    Cuts the sphere of the world in two!
But oh! she has reached the nearer ring,
    And is unmolested still!
And she sails along with the doleful song,
    " Ah, me, I have failed to kill!"

One, two, three ! and she falls again,
    And she says to Sir Trout, " O pray
Don't let me escape as my sister did,
    Who passed just now this way ! "
But ah ! that she thus comes sailing on,
    Proves that the prayer was vain !
Sir Trout is at least of doubtful mind ;
    Well, well, let us try him again !

One, two, three !- not a shade of doubt
    That the fly is right to a shade !
Nor more like that he is rising at
    Could any quill-gnat be made !
So now, my friend, like an auctioneer,
    I'll wait for your little bid !
'Tis going, going, going—*gone !*
    Ha ! ha !—'twas well I did !

So ho ! so ho ! Don't hurry away
    With my goods to your weedy home,
Like a common thief !—there's the bill to pay !
    So come, my beauty, come !
So ho ! hysterics are out of place !
    Let me lead you gently, so !
Ha ! would you escape ? turn back, my friend,
    That isn't the way to go !

So ho! so ho! You're faint, I see,
   And needing a little rest!
Here's a nice little room, will fit you well,
   In which you may make your nest!
Don't make such a fuss! lie down, lie down!
   That's better! come here to me
On this grassy bank, and hear from my lips
   How proud I am of thee!

NORTH COUNTRY FLY-FISHING.

Let your Southron stand with rod in hand,
   Fishing as in a dream,
In his one green meadow, the morning long,
   By his clear, still, chalky stream ;
But ever let me in the North Countree,
   Wander my burn beside,
Where it winds thro' the mead and the rocky gorge,
   And the moorland wild and wide !

No thresher am I of the vexèd air,
   Or your quiet, mantling pools,
Who stands for an hour on the same green sod,
   'Mid a crowd of gaping fools ;
Changing each little failing fly,
   Till all in his book are tried ;
My one good cast for a day will last ;
   And on with my wand I stride !

Stretcher and dropper, one, two, three, four,
    With flies of various hue—
Meeting the taste of the connoisseur
    With yellow, green, brown, or blue—
I fling, with a shortened line, across
    The swirling, eddying burn,
Drawing them tenderly toward my bank,
    With a delicate-handed turn.

They sink, and they swirl, and I cannot see
    My flies; but my hand can feel,
My hands are the eyes that see the rise,
    My vision is in my reel!
Let the Southron look, like a boy on his book,
    For his still-stream, dimpled ring;
'Tis the hand that can *see* in the North Countree,
    And *hear* when the reel doth sing!

I feel the pulse of the burn's bent arm,
    Where it lies on the gravelly strand;
And under the shade of the beechen boughs,
    I deftly ply my wand;
But most I love the eddying pools
    At the foot of the rock-toss'd foam,
For the fat and the fair of the stream are there
    For morning calls " at home! "

Thus on I go from shallow to pool,
   And from pool to shallow again !
And all is change, and all is life,
   Moor, meadow and gorge and glen !
Thus, keeping step with my flowing burn,
   My happy moments steal,
And ne'er do I pause, save when I've cause
   To add to my filling creel.

THE WARY OLD TROUT CAUGHT WITH A SALMON FLY.

[Suggested by the following passage from "My First Salmon Run," by Mr. Francis Francis:—"I fished on down to the end of the cast, and got a dashing rise, but I found it was only a big yellow trout, of three pounds, which I very soon disposed of with a certain amount of contempt, and yet when trout fishing I had tried that trout most carefully with a variety of lures over and over again, for I knew him well, and many a time my heart had been in my mouth as he came up cautiously, and critically inspected my fly or minnow, and then with a wave of his tail, expressive of his contempt for it, retreated to his watery fastness; and yet to-day, because I chanced to be after salmon, I looked on him as inferior ware, while he, who had so cautiously looked into moderate offers, and reasonable four or five per cent. bargains, where he had a fair chance of getting off with bait and all for a scrape, like a rash speculator, thinking he could realise ten or fifteen per cent., with limited liability, risked his all in one mad rush and lost it. Verily, the world of fishes may be likened unto that of humanity in many respects."]

I OFT had seen in Whammle-foot
　　A large and shapely trout,
And, with adapted lure, had tried
　　In vain to coax him out;
I match'd the flies I knew he loved,
　　I plied my utmost skill;
I rose him oft, but all in vain—
　　That trout I could not kill!

But once I went to Whammle-foot
    Nor seeking trout, nor wishing
To see my friend ; far lordlier game
    Was sought in that day's fishing :
My cast a many-coloured fly,
    And large, had on to gammon.
By all the skill that art could ply,
    Some splendid silver salmon.

Nor less than three that glorious day
    My 'prentice hand had caught ;
And now I reach'd my trout's old home,
    Yet gave him not a thought,
Nor wish ; when whistle went my reel—
    Said I, " What luck's about ?
Another salmon ? "   Ah, I'd got
    At last, and thus, my trout !

As thus with fish, so oft with men—
    Temptations plied with skill
To meet their taste, will often fail
    Their eye with lust to fill ;
While baits, that seem for them too gross,
    Prove oft the fatal spell
That takes their eyes with quick surprise,
    And lures them into hell !

DREAM-FISHING.

When languor lays her downy palm
   On eyes by sickness rendered dim ;
Or when in health I want a balm
   To soothe, apart from prayer or hymn ;
When tardy sleep delays to seal
   The brain that vainly seeks repose,
I love by night away to steal
   To where the Test meandering flows ;

Or where the Coln, my boyhood's love,
   Flows down the breezy Cotswold hills ;
Or willowy Isis cools the grove
   That waves beside her placid rills ;
Or where the Wandle slowly winds
   Her weedy way ; or dimpling Dee
Fills Cynwyd's vale ; or alder binds
   The daisied banks of Walton's Lea ;

Where Darenth creeps thro' park and lawn,
   And dallies with the lily bells ;
Where sluggish Avon, slowly drawn,
   Thro' flowery flats, barge-laden swells ;

Or arrowy Dart thro' branchy woods
    O'er rock and boulder cleaves her way;
Or stately Thames, the Queen of floods,
    Doth round green eyots laughing play;

Or where the Aar coils snakelike thro'
    The glooming hills of lone Nassau;
Or Thun's deep lake of lucent blue
    Reflects the snowy Silber-Frau;*
Or where the broad Muotta speeds †
    Her wild way with a sparkling glee;
Or where thro' blood-stained Norman meads‡
    The Arques flows softly to the sea.

And there in fancy o'er and o'er
    To live sweet spring and summer days
By river, brook, or lakelet shore,
    O'er sunny streams or shaded bays,
And all my hope and all my fear
    And all my joy again to feel
And—climax of my joy--to hear
    Re-play the music of the reel.

* The Jungfrau's peak is named the Silber-horn.
† The Muotta flows through the Canton Schwyz, and falls into the Lac des Quatre Cantons at Brunnen.
‡ The Arques flows through the battle-field where Henri Quatre defeated the League.

In turns by each I walk or sit,
    And throw the fly or watch the float.
While Memory, with her lamp, relit,
    Past incidents of sport doth note—
Ah, *here* what royal battles fought
    With leaping trout, or bream or dace!
Ah, *there* no fish I ever caught!
    Blank days that time will ne'er efface!

Yet still 'tis sweet to live again
    Those various days in changeful dreams,
Those peaceful, happy seasons when
    I fished these well-beloved streams,
And thus to find in fancy flights
    Relief, while memory backward strays,
And hours of pain and winter nights
    Are cheered by suns of other days.

TO HADDON HALL.

SEAR'D, grey, old pile, embalmed by hoary Time,
More reverend now than in thy living prime,
When pulsed thine angelus' sweet evening chime!

For now can Fancy play around thy towers,
And in her magic light thy halls and bowers
People with squire and dame of antique hours.

She sees in sunshine of the summers gone
Young eyes that in those woodbined oriels shone
Scan the far meads for some belovèd one.

Anon they meet—she with her golden hair,
The hooded falcon on her wrist so fair,
To seek the heron in his reedy lair.

Then Fancy dreams, and in her dreams she sees
The sequel of those tender courtesies,
And all the bridal's gay festivities.

Led by her lord, the bride with gentle grace
Curtseys adieu, and rides for Ensor Place,*
While Fancy turns and rests a little space.

* Edensor, so usually abbreviated, adjoining Chatsworth.

Then sees the chaplain in his serge and hood
Perch'd on the greensward in a musing mood
Angle for grayling in Wye's gentle flood.

She sees the monks in long procession pass,
To say in Bakewell's fane the Whitsun mass,
Bared peasants kneeling on the wayside grass.

Night falls ; thy warriors deckt with lance and plume,
Returning victors from some field of doom,
File o'er thy bridge while flambeaux light the gloom.

Cheers for thy conquering lord the yeoman calls,
While mailèd warriors on thy turret walls
Hoist sign of welcome to his joyous halls.

The windows glow ; below the feast is spread :
The wassail bowl is shared, the dancers tread
A measure to the harp till dawn flames red.

Thus as in Rowsley meads I fling the fly,
And in my sport thine ivied towers pass by,
These old-world visions crowd on Memory's eye ;

And rapt Imagination doth impart
" Hues of her own fresh borrowed from the heart,"
That give a tenfold pleasure to my art.

The winding Wye would ever beauteous glide
Had'st thou unbuilt ne'er been his joy and pride,
But O, the loss wert thou not by his side !

Song—*THE ANGLER AND THE BROOK.*

THE west wind wafts the scent of May
  Adown the verdant valleys;
The friendly sun with temper'd ray
  Peers forth from cloudy alleys,
And in his gleams, the duns and browns
  In joy of life are winging,
While I, afar from noisy towns,
  Go forth to angle singing.

Anon the music of the brook
  Sounds near in happy chorus;
Her beaming face with laughing look
  Sings, O the joy before us!
I greet her with a look as bright,
  And wave my wand above her;
She glances coy, pretending fright,
  Yet knows me for her lover.

Thro' cowslip meadows, side by side,
  We wander, fondly clinging
Each unto each, like groom and bride,
  No turns estrangement bringing;

And many a gold and coral gem
    She takes from out her bosom,
And, proud, at eve she gives me them,
    Beneath the hawthorn's blossom.

I stoop and kiss her pure, sweet lips,
    And mine she softly presses,
Then turns aside, and shyly dips
    Beneath her drooping tresses;
Then babbling on in laughing glee,
    Assumed to hide her sorrow,
She pauses 'neath a willow-tree,
    And sings, Return to-morrow!

Song—THE OLD BROOK REVISITED.

How changed, how changed, how little changed !
  Myself and these dear haunts of eld :
These fields, where I a schoolboy ranged ;
  Not one familiar tree is fell'd ;
'Tis all the same—the garden wall
  Blooms with the selfsame blossoms still ;
The old brook murmuring round the Hall,
    Seeks still the same old water-mill.
      Oh, changed ! oh, changed ! yet little changed !
      'O earth ! O sky ! how little changed !

How changed ! how changed ! Years twice a score
  Have left their various marks on me ;
The playmates of those days of yore—
  How many dead, or o'er the sea !
And some that live now pass me by,
  Not knowing, or with hearts estranged ;
Ah ! mid this unchanged scene I sigh,—
    How much is changed ! how much is changed !
      How changed, where all seems little changed !
      O days ! O years, how much is changed !

                                                        I

Ay, tho' this old grey pile doth know
  No more its ancient lord or ways,
'Tis so the same in outward show,
  That forty years seem yesterdays :
The same—yet not the same : 'tis so
  With me ; this strange self's outer part
How changed ! yet these old loves that glow
  As memory wakens, prove the heart
    But little changed, but little changed
      By changing years, how little changed !

Song—*THE WATER REAPERS.*

The reapers of the streams are we,
  A free and favoured band,
And who will dare with us compare
  The reapers of the land?
They reap but once 'neath Autumn suns,
' When corn is ripe and sere,
But we reap all the seasons four,
  Our harvest-time's the year.
          The water reapers then are we,
            A blest and favored band,
          And who will dare with us compare
            The reapers of the land?

A golden harvest oft we reap,
  Ere green hath tipp'd the thorn ;
When Summer flaunts her gayest robe,
  When Winter sighs forlorn ;

And oft we reap beneath the moon,
　　Nor need we summer weather ;
And find our crops mid barren hills,
　　Wild moor and purple heather.
　　　　The water reapers then are we,
　　　　　A free, unfettered band,
　　　　And who will dare with us compare
　　　　　The reapers of the land ?

We reap the waters with a hook,
　　As they, but, strange to say,
We thrash our harvest ere we reap,
　　In a topsy turvey way ;
Our spoil doth rise, while theirs doth fall.
　　And unresisting yields,
But battle's zest and battle's chance
　　Attend our reaping fields.
　　　　Brave water reapers then are we,
　　　　　A stalwart, gallant band,
　　　　And who will dare with us compare
　　　　　The reapers of the land ?

Our flails are light as Ariel's wand,
　　Our reaping hooks so small,
You cannot see their sweeping stroke,
　　Or hear their fateful fall ;

They fly about the reaping field
  On light and airy wing,
And when they bear their burden home
  Their " Harvest Home " they ring,
      O water reapers strange are we,
        A fairy, airy band,
      And who will dare with us compare
      The reapers of the land ?

More independent far are we
  Than reapers of the soil
Who sweat all day in one small field
  With weary, changeless toil,
While we roam free o'er moor and lea,
  And need no barn nor stack,
Since, free as air, we lightsome bear
  Our garners on our back.
      O water reapers free are we,
        An independent band,
      And who will dare with us compare
      The reapers of the land ?

SONG FOR THE ANNUAL DINNER OF THE FLY-FISHERS' CLUB.

Stern winter o'er the streams we love,
    Now holds his rigid sway;
The banks where we were wont to roam
    Are leafless, bare and grey;
But here around the social board
    To him we'll not succumb,
But joy o'er Memory's vernal hoard
    And hope for Mays to come!

Let friendship be a summer sun
    To cheer us with its ray,
And smile to smile electric run
    To turn our night to day;
And while we cast our looks around,
    As on the stream our flies,
Let heart to heart in gladsome bound
    And kindly greeting rise.

The water will unloose our tongue,
  Without the aid of wine ;
The rod, now like a bow unstrung,
  Will bend above our line ¡
As here we sing of singing reels,
  Or talk of loch and stream,
And of our full or empty creels,
  In this midwinter dream.

And should a tear drop in the cup,
  O'er all our angler's woes,
O let us bravely drink it up
  And all sad themes foreclose !
Our gentle art hath ways, no doubt,
  That tempt our wrath to rise ;
But let us not to-night hatch out
  Such joy-disturbing flies !

TO THE SUN.

ON A SPRING-LIKE DAY IN JANUARY.

O GLORIOUS sun, after days so dun,
    What bliss thy brightness brings!
Beneath my ribs there's a tremulous stir
    Like a flutter of inward wings:
The sap in my limbs like a pulse doth beat,
    Like the leaf-germ in the thorn;
While a muffled music throbs in my heart
    Like a lark in the egg, unborn.

I fancy I see the daisies stir
    In the meadows beneath thy beams;
While, watching for flies that they feel must rise,
    Trout quiver their fins in the streams;
I long to grasp my rod in thy ray,
    And play on my sleeping reel,
For spite of winter, the feelings of spring
    Illusively o'er me steal.

No Persian bows in thy brilliant beam,
    Adoring thy face divine,
In a rapture of worship, beholding thee,
    With a joy surpassing mine!

I could mount to kiss thy glowing brow
   If these unformed wings would grow,
To show what I feel of grateful love
   For the bliss thou givest below.

O, servant of God ! that gathering cloud
   On thy face my words would ban,
As Peter the prostrate soldier check'd—
   " Rise up, for I, too, am a man ! "
" Not Giver, but only Apostle to bring
   From my Maker these gladdening rays."
Apostle, I hail thee ! and with thee give
   To the Great Sunmaker praise !

MEADOW MISTS IN THE GLOAMING.

When o'er the silver-sheeted stream
    Sad eve her glooming shadow throws,
I wander in a pensive dream
    While memory's backward current flows.

And as I pace my homeward way
    Amid the hushed and tranquil scene,
The meadow mists that gliding stray
    Seem ghosts of friends that here have been;

Of friends this stream and I have known
    In days—ah, happy days!—of yore
Who here the mimic fly have thrown
    But throw it now, alas, no more!

Those poplars mark the reach called "Grey";
    His favorite spot his name receives;
As upright he in soul as they,
    And tender as their trembling leaves.

And there's the cot of keeper Giles ;
  He, too, is in the shadow land !
Good honest soul ! his cheery smiles
  Still seem to greet me where I stand.

Yon alder o'er thy favorite pool,
  Brings back my Arthur, best of friends !
Thy matchless cast which fell like wool ;
  Thy rod's unequall'd sweeps and bends.

And now from out yon bower withdrawn,
  Comes back thy cheery, ringing laugh,
As when above the eggs and brawn,
  The king trout's health we used to quaff.

I pass the thatch with low bared head,
  Saluting sadly thus thy shade,
Nor ever, O belovèd dead,
  The memory of those days shall fade !

Ah me ! beside this silent mill
  I see another, seen no more ;
His graceful rod seems waving still,
  As ere he fell, Maiwand before !

There waved his sword as waved his rod,
  With brave, broad sweep o'er victims slain
Now sleeps he 'neath the Afghan sod,
  Nor rod, nor sword shall sweep again !

Thus as the river floweth by
  My homeward path, where'er I gaze,
Some spirit meets sad memory's eye,
  To " mind me of departed days."

The river only is the same !
  We tread awhile its marge and fade,
And, leaving none, or but a name,
  We pass into the silent shade.

A MODERN ST. ANTHONY'S
SERMON TO FISHES.*

On " the Lust of the Flesh, the Lust of the Eyes, and the Pride
of Life."

Ye who casting downward vision,
Grope and grovel in the mud,
Water-swine of oozes Stygian,
Dull of brain and black of blood.
Hating, fearing light of Heaven,
Finding bliss in foulest deeps,
Gross with flesh desire doth leaven,
Brothers of the worm that creeps :
Beware desire, beware desire !
That winsome morsel ye admire
Is devil-sunk before your eyes,
To charm you into Death's surprise !

---

* Our predecessor in this style of preaching was St. Anthony, of
Vieyre, in Spain, whose celebrated "Sermon to Fishes" is well-
known. It need hardly be added that that was in prose. St.
Anthony was one of the keenest wits and satirists of his age, and
his great gift of humour was used to the noblest ends.

Ye who roam the weedy sedges,
  Or in dozing, dreamful ease,
Bask beneath the lily ledges,
  Shaded by the summer trees,
Greedy, grasping, never sharing,
  Preying on your weaker kin
Wrapt in self, nor ever caring
  Who may lose, so you may win :
Beware desire, beware desire !
Or, tho' ye rise above the mire,
Some barbèd gaud may tempt your eye,
On Death suspicionless to fly.

Ye whom nobler aspiration
  Saves from grossness, mud, and slime,
Scorning deeps of degradation,
  Skyward lifting eyes sublime,
Ranging clearer, purer waters,
  O'er whose bosom fancy-flies,
Summer's fairy-footed daughters
  Robed in beauty, fall and rise ;
Beware desire, beware desire !
Beware her soul-propelling fire !
Under Beauty's gauzy wing
Death conceals his barbèd sting !

BROKEN LINES AND DOUBLES ENTENTES.

A RIVERSIDE REVERIE.

I NEVER can that hour forget,
  And dear to me the very place is,
When first at Vivian Place we met,—
  What memories that sweet name embraces !—
She sweetly sang ; I praised the song ;
  Her pleasèd smile went thro' and thro' me,
Nor could I sleep the whole night long—
          That rise was to me !

I went to Vivian Place next day,
  On some pretence that love invented,
And chanced to meet her on the way,
  And spoke, confused and half demented ;
Recall'd the song with praise, and she
  Fearing my praise would come too thickly,
Was rather stiff—becomingly—
          I struck too quickly !

I took the hint ; it did me good ;
 I stay'd away a month lamenting;
I let her see I understood
 My fault, and sadly was repenting ;
And she, I found, grew guarded too,
 Nor walk'd but with her sister Connie,
Lest meeting me, I might renew—
     'Ware ! " Steady, Johnny ! "

I too assumed a proud reserve,
 Concealing love 'neath outward coldness,
And seemed unworthy to deserve
 Her notice since my former boldness;
I carried roses in my hand
 To make her fear my heart was ranging,
Yet tried to make her understand—
     That fly wants changing !

I then sincerer tactics tried,
 And went to pay a call, and surely
I met her—Connie by her side—
 They bow'd and pass'd, and look'd demurely ;
She said, " He shall not think me flirt,
 So with reserve let us accost him,"—
My love was pain'd ; my pride was hurt—
     O, almost lost him !

But still, methought, that tender flush
 That mantled on her cheek had meaning :
Mere scorn could ne'er so sweetly blush ;
 Scorn never had such gentle screening ;
It gave me hope ; it gave me cheer ;
 'Twas plainly writ down in my duty,
With caution still to persevere—
 You're mine, my beauty ! *

I now grew bolder, she less shy,
 Some little coyness notwithstanding,
And soon--dear Connie *not* being by--
 We came unto an understanding,
And sealed it with a kiss and vow,
 That evermore by Hymen banded,
Our hearts should be—as they are now—
 Ha ! safely landed!

* See page 130.

K

"MY BEAUTY."*

SONG. THE OLD ANGLER TO HIS WIFE.

I CALLED thee " my beauty " when first in our youth,
We pledged to each other our love and our truth,
And I felt there were none in the ranks of the fair
That could with " my beauty " one moment compare;
But how small was the part of the beauty revealed
To the beauty within that thy beauty concealed.

And O, with what joy, what elation and pride,
I called thee " my beauty " arrayed as my bride,
When I felt that thy beauty would gladden my life
In the form of my good and my beautiful wife;
And the years as they rolled with their good and their
    ill,
Revealed some new beauty more beautiful still!

* See last line of stanza 6, page 130.

O, those years, ah, how many, "my beauty," have
    flown !
They are counted by birthdays of children upgrown ;
They have left the sad traces of trial and care,
And many a sorrow hath silvered thy hair ;
But, altho' the fresh bloom of thy youth is no more,
Thou art *now* more " my beauty " than ever before !

ODE.

QUEEN of the Island-Realm,
   Vein'd with the silver streams
That flow thro' England's verdant meads,
   Like songs thro' poet's dreams;
And circled by the seas,
   Where Britain's navies ride—
Those that thy throne and people guard,
   These that their wealth provide!

Not *those* engage to-day
   Thy royal heart and mind,
But *these* that brave the stormy wave
   The finny food to find;
Not those that flash in fire
   To make thy foemen flee,
But these that thro' the fields of blue
   Sail out to reap the sea!

These that encounter death
  To reap a living store ;
Nor thro' the wrack do all come back
  To harvest-home ashore !
Their sorrows on the sea
  They know thy heart doth share,
For Science, Art, and Law thou bid'st
  For their protection care.

No booming guns of war
  Shake in thy praise the skies,
But manly cheers from lowly ships
  Of Peace and Plenty rise !
Britannia's Fisher-Fleet,
  Prow pointed towards this scene,
Their gracious Queen salutes to-day,
  And these salute their Queen !

But since thy flag doth float
  Supreme on every sea,
Thy heart salutes the total main
  In blest Philanthropy !
The Fisher-world is one,
  Whate'er its various name,
And here to-day with heart and voice
  Unites in one acclaim !

LANDSCAPE WITH CATTLE :
DEESIDE.

[Drawn from life—personal

THE dappled cattle on the lea,
Beside the lonely banks of Dee,
How beautiful they are to see
    As Cooper limns them !
How pleasing when Jean Ingelow
Doth make them in soft numbers low,
Their plaintive moan is music so
    As poet hymns them !

How meekly do they stand and dream,
Knee-deep in the pellucid stream,
Or chew the cud to make our cream,
    As bard hath sung them,
Or painter to the eye doth bring !
But ye that paint and ye that sing,
'Tis oft a very different thing
    To be among them !—

Among them in a hot July,
'Neath the sun's fierce, unclouded eye.
When they are galled by heat and fly.
    If angler passes,
He'll get a stare from all their eyes
That will his fearsome soul surprise.
And bring to view an unsought *rise*
    Among the grasses !

So pass'd I once along a mead,
On either side of which did feed
A herd : and each a bull did lead,
    And both were roaring!
And, hot with wrath, their tails did switch :
Behind me was a hopeless ditch ;
Before—the Dee ! my choice was, which—
    Drowning or goring ?

These two detectives at each gate
O'erleaned, my coming to await,
And on me in my piteous state
    Turn'd both their bull's eyes !
They meant to " run me in " 'twas clear !
What could I do but cry, oh, dear ?
For, tho' no coward, yet my fear
    Had grown to full size!

At last, one bull, to cool his rage,
Sought Dee's mid-stream, his thirst t'assuage,
While I crept from my verdant cage
          And leaped the five-barr'd !
And, while he drank, I cross'd the mead,
Like one who, caught in evil deed,
Eluding " Bobby " with all speed,
          Cries, " Cabby, drive hard ! "

Then just as " Bobby " stop thief ! cries—
The bull roars out, as quick he spies
My flying form !   With dread surprise
          I hear his bellow !
And that more awful, fateful sound,
His thundering hoofs most dread rebound
Behind me shake the trembling ground,
Nor dared I pause to look around,
For fear did all my sense confound,
When safety just in time I found,
And, breathless as a winded hound,
And nearly fainting in a swound,
Cried, as I sank upon a mound,
          O lucky fellow !

PART IV.

FISHERMEN.

ISYS TO IZAAK

ON THE BI-CENTENARY OF HIS DEATH, DEC. 15, 1883.

GREAT master who did'st first impart
That passion for the gentle art
Which puls'd within my youthful heart,
    I wish, for thy sake,
That sweet, idyllic, pastoral muse
Which shed on thee Castalian dews,
Would into this my song infuse
    Thy soul, good *Izaak*.

While to thyself I fain would pay
The homage of a worthy lay !
Then, hearken, muse, as thus I pray,
    And Attic salt on
My verse, so burdened, sprinkle ! deign
To breathe thine influence on the strain
That would some lofty note attain
    In praise of *Walton !*

Thy name, O Walton 's like a breeze
Of summer thro' the alder trees,
Breathing sweet country fragrances ;
    While thy pure pages

Are like those sheets of linen prime,
Perfum'd with lavender and thyme,
That wrapt thy bed, and scent thy rhyme
  And prose for ages.

Reading thy page, we seem to see
And hear thy "scholar" chat with thee,
As toward thy much-lov'd river *Lea*
  Ye gaily trot on ;
Or still beside the banks of *Dove*,
The river of thine equal love,
Behold ye as ye fish and rove.
  Thyself and *Cotton*.*

Wherein doth lie that nameless spell
That in thy charmèd style doth dwell ?
'Tis found in one sweet syllable—
  Love !—love, not lucre
Nor fame, but love inspired thy pen,
Whether it wrote of fish or men,
When fish to hook, its theme ; or when
  " *The Life of Hooker*."†

---

 * Cotton was, as is well-known, Walton's great friend. Their fishing-house still stands on the banks of the Dove, with their interwoven monogram carved in stone over the door. Cotton wrote a second part to "The Complete Angler," and the two parts are generally bound up together.
 † Izaak Walton was the author of "The Life of Richard Hooker," the great Church of England divine.

Above two centuries thy word*
Hath hovered like the holy bird ;
And still thy calming voice is heard
    'Mid strife and jostle :
Thou art as to the wheel the grease ;
Like balm that bids the fever cease,
The Laureate of holy peace,
    Content's Apostle.

Wise but not dull; tho' grave yet gay ;
Sober as Autumn, bright as May :
Of fishing lore thou art for aye
    The Senior Wrangler;
Wit fills thy head, and grace thy heart ;
Or wielding rod or pen, thou art
Unrivall'd, and in every part
    A " *Complete Angler.*"†

O life to envy, course and close !
As calm and white as alpine snows,
Yet bloomy-bright as summer rose
    Sweet odours rich in !
Be " Requiescat ! " fondly said
Above thy venerable head,
Which lies in fit, sepulchral bed
    Beside *the Itchen !*‡

---

* He was born in 1593 and died in 1683.
† The title of his celebrated work.
‡ He lies buried in Winchester Cathedral, near to the famous trout stream so named.

THE TERCENTENARY OF IZAAK
WALTON.

Written at the request of R. B. Marston, Esq., Editor of *The Fishing Gazette*, and read at the celebration in Walton's honour, at Broxbourne, August 9th, 1893, at which he was chairman.

A HUSH, a solemn hush, one moment now,
   Amid these festive rites so glad and gay,
While we to Walton's name uncovered bow,
   And to his memory reverent homage pay;
And where more fitly could such ritual be
Than on the banks of his beloved Lea?

The Lea that shared with his and Cotton's Dove
   And Itchen (by whose meadowed banks he lies),
And Shawford brook, his almost equal love,
   And, for his sake, our own fond sympathies;
The Lea whose name, while anglers cast a line,
Will with his memory ever intertwine.

Flow on, thou sacred river, now so changed
   Since he beside thee heard the milkmaid's song,
Or chatted with Venator as they ranged
   Thy meads unvexed as yet by pleasure's throng;

Flow on, for thou, at least in Fancy's dream,
Art, like Illissus, an immortal stream.

Aye, tho' no more the honeysuckle blows
   Beside those streams which now the otter shuns,
Tho' those fair fields where Aucep's falcon rose
   See only sparrows for suburban guns ;
Tho' where the haymead perfumed Tottenham Cross,
Small factory urchins play at pitch and toss.*

Three changeful centuries have now gone by
   Since honoured Stafford gave him vital breath†
And generations ten have wearily
   Paced by the milestones on the way to death ;
But Walton is not dead : he still is here
In power that groweth from bright year to year.

" My odes," sang Horace, " are my monument
   Ære perennius, tho' my body die," ‡
And in sweet prose of Nature's ornament,
   Walton hath wrought his immortality :
For letters live when brass and stone decay,
And these are dumb, but those will speak for aye.

———

* The reference is of course to the lower reaches of the Lea.
† He was born at Stafford August 9th, 1593.
‡ *Exegi monumentum ære perennius*—I have raised for myself
a monument more lasting than brass.

The one and ninety years of Walton's life
   Pass'd in an atmosphere of fevered qualm,
Yet he could angle and forget the strife,
   And sing and write as in a halcyon calm ;
Faction and civil war did round him rage,
But who would guess it from his tranquil page?

What owe we, brethren, to that tome so pure
   Whose leaves breathe inspiration and have breathed?
How many here did Izaak first allure
   To stream and pool and pleasures thus bequeathed?
Pleasures so pure no other sport can show,
Which those who never angle never know.

Pleasures that make us kinder to our kind,
   And teach us sweet content 'neath clouds of care,
That soften manners and refine the mind,
   And lift the musing heart to praise and prayer:
No Kenna* weeps sad tears, but sings a song,
If to an angler doth her heart belong.

Long live and flourish then our gentle art,
   And gentle-men may his disciples be
Who on life's stage so nobly played his part,
   And left behind this fragrant memory !
O sacred shade ! may thine be worthy thee !
And hark !—Amen ! comes whispering from the Lea.

---

   * His pet name for his second wife, the sister of Bishop Ken, the author of the following hymn :—
   "Here, hear my Kenna sing a song." *The Angler's Wish.*

A WREATH OF TRIBUTE.

IN MEMORIAM: FRANCIS FRANCIS.

If life hath now an added store
  Of bliss, and grief hath less of pain,
  And poverty a wealth of gain
Undreamt of in the days before

That page was read that brought to view
  The varied pleasures of the field,
  The joys that lake and river yield,
Bright as May suns and pure as dew—

That page that manly vigour breathes
  And glows with passion that inspires
  Who reads with all the love that fires
Itself—is it not meet that wreaths

Of tribute from their hands who learn'd
  From Francis Francis first to love
  The anglers art, should hang above
The tomb where now he lies intern'd,

L

˙That fitting tomb beside the banks
   His much-lov'd Thames doth.sadly lave,
   In life his home, in death his grave)
Mutely to murmur grateful thanks?

ON READING "DAYS IN DOVEDALE BY THE AMATEUR ANGLER."

CHEERY, chatty, breezy booklet,
  Breathing scents of wilding flowers,
Cool and clear as mountain brooklet,
Yet diffusing warmth of sunshine
  Thro' these wintry hours :

Whence the power thy artless pages
  Have to soothe my weary brain,
Killing cares that Wisdom's sages,
Plying philosophic maxims.
  Reason with in vain ?

Hence :—because, like him thou ownest
  With such modest grace, thy king,*
To the heart that's saddest. lonest,
Needing healing. thou dost simply
  Nature's simples bring.

* Izaak Walton.

Nature's simples, God's specific,
    Pure and sweet as Cana's wine ;
Flowing from His hand benefic,
Fresh, by art left uncorrupted,
    Living blood of vine !—

Making glad man's heart and lifting
    From it all its weight of care,
Till its sorrows seem like drifting
Clouds that fly before the rising
    Of a mountain air.

Thanks for such a breeze, O writer,
    Blown from thy pure page to-night !
Night without its darkness, brighter
Far than common days, for with thee
    I have walk'd in light :

Shared thy hope whilst thou hast angled,
    Nor could help a laugh to see
All thy woes with line entangled,
All thy flyless whippings, and thy
    Flight from angry bee !

Felt a sympathetic sadness
    With thy disappointments ; seen
With delight that sight of gladness—
Age and infancy together
    Romping on the green !

O, with Lorna and with Alice,
　Far from stir and strife of men,
Rod in hand, refill thy chalice
In the dales of Dove, and often
　Prythee write again !

" OLD TIMBERTOES,"

OF TWEEDSIDE: A RIVERSIDE SKETCH.

[See Henderson's " My Life as an Angler," p. 273.]

" Jock, who's he that stands so still
In those rushing waters chill,
Statue-like, and flinging flies
O'er each dimpling, circling rise;
Lacking waders, while his knees
Sink in water there to freeze ;
Icicles his legs must be,
Who, good Jock, say, who is he ? "

" Wha?— 'tis he all Tweedside knows
By the name of ' Timbertoes ' :
Wanting feet and wanting legs.
Stands he on twa wooden pegs :
Nay, upon a *third* that fits
Like a tail, he leans or sits,
Snug as in the ingle-close,
Doughty, tough old Timbertoes !

Legs of larches make him bold,
Naught like wood to stand the cold !
Waders he can scorn in glee,
Waterproof himself is he !
Feareth he no colds, I wis,
Corns or gout or ' rheumatiz ! '
Be the water cold as snows,
Ne'er a chill feels Timbertoes ! "

" Jock, that is a joke indeed !
Sure he's Neptune o' the Tweed !
Tho' to him, old Nep's a goose :
His a tripod turned to use !
Canny Scot, not pagan fool,
Tim converts it to a stool !
Bravo ! free from foes and woes,
Fish and flourish, Timbertoes ! "

HIS WORST FOE.

A THRENODY.

I KNOW not how it is with you,
   O brethren of the angle,
When in debate on angler's foes
   You feel disposed to wrangle;
I fancy one might say, Eyed hooks!
   Another, Tackle-makers!
And one, American split canes!
   And others, River stakers!

Or one might say, Sham silken lines!
   Another, Lawn-weed-sweepers!
While some in wrath, The river launch!
   And some, The River-keepers!
But would ye ask your humble bard
   To view them all together,
And say which *he* has found the worst,
   He'd say at once—The Weather!

He knows too well the foes you name,
  And much has suffered from them,
Nor wonders that your righteous wrath
  Would wish a shell to bomb them ;
But in his own experience strange
  He vows by young Apollo,
That that dire foe he now has named
  Beats all the others hollow.

This very day—'tis sober fact,
  And not a poet's fiction—
When I would go to Darenth's stream,
  My foe gave contradiction ;
I rose at six, elate with hope,
  But he rose up before me,
And roared from out the north of east
  Like angry bull to gore me !

And here I am in fishing boots,
  And flies within my pocket,
His vanquished foe ! while he looks on
  My woeful face to mock it—
That vile nor'-easter who six times
  Before, this year, I vow, sir,
Hath spoiled my sport, or kept me in
  As ruthlessly as now, sir !

And yet it is not *March* when one
  Might well expect to hear him
Thus bellow from his icy throat,
  And reasonably fear him ;
But mark ! it is the midst of *May*,
  When one might look for zephyrs,
And not a roar like that one hears
  Within the caves of Pfeffers.

But, such my luck, I do believe,
  If I should say in August
" I'll start to fish," he'd say, " You shan't !"
  And brew at once a raw gust
I know that some days must be bad,
  Nor wait upon *my* wishing,
But oh, 'tis strange the bad days come
  Just then when I go fishing !

In short, of all the luckless sons
  Of men that rod hath wielded,
I must maintain the most am I
  Who now to fate hath yielded !
I give it up ! " Blow all ye winds,
  And crack your cheeks !" I'm mad, Sirs,
Like poor old Lear ! If you've more luck,
  For *your* sakes, then, I'm glad, Sirs !

DEE-CEITS AND DEE-LUSIONS.

WE came to Dee one hot July
And hoped for splendid angling,
But with us disappointment came
To give our hopes a mangling;
For, soon as we arrived, we heard
"The time for Dee is over,
You'd now catch trout almost as soon
From off the pier at Dover!"

We find the river all extremes.
'Tis or too dull or bright thing;
'Tis now too high; 'tis now too low;
It never is the right thing!
And every stream around's the same.
Success we never shall win,
For, sure as fate, there's something wrong
Whene'er we fish the Alwen.

We try for grayling, then we hear
To-day those fish are ailing!
We try for trout, and then are told
We should have fish'd for grayling!

We try the lake, and then they say
  " They'd on the river take well ;"
Next day the river, then we hear
  " They rose upon the lake well! "

Whene'er we spinning-minnows take
  There is a splendid *rise*, sir ;
When we take flies, the fish take worms,
  When worms, they fancy flies, sir ;
Thus all we do for right is wrong,
  Dame Fortune won't befriend us ;
Wind, weather, water, fish, and flies
  Conspire bad luck to send us !

And when at eve we notes compare
  With some successful brother,
We find the flies we used were wrong,
  We should have tried—some other !
" And how long did you fish? "   " 'Till three,
  Then home till eve we wended."
" The very hour the rise began,
  And just at five it ended ! "

We thought the fishing free, but found
  Subscription tickets needed,
Tho' many fish who do not pay ;
  Perhaps we're fools that we did !

We brought no stockings waterproof,
  Nor thought that Dee invaders
Demanded for success ; but find
  No chance except for waders !

Our patience needs for worthy praise
  The pen that writes evangels ;
And could you see our merriment,
  You'd say, we're more than angels ;
For jovial are we under all
  That turns out thus mishaply,
And quite as jolly under woe
  As ever was Mark Tapley !

THE HOUSEWARMING OF THE FLY-FISHERS' CLUB

On removing to the Arundel Hotel, Adelphi, July 12th, 1888.

AROUND the festal board, at once to warm
    Our hearts and new-found home, we gathered gaily,
To honour him whose genius first did form
    The Club where anglers may assemble daily,
—Harbour of refuge from domestic storm—
    Where friend greets friend with *Ave* or with *Vale* ;
And there, like needles, magnetised by worth
We pointed steadfast to the trusty *North.**

Adelphians of the rod that flings the fly
    To lure the lordly salmon, trout or grayling,
We wish'd to show our founder loyally
    That lack of gratitude was not our failing,

          * The Hon. Sir Ford North was in the chair.

That, *au contraire*, we anglers ever try
  To honour merit that deserves unveiling,
Like *his*, forsooth, whose secretarial skill
  Rose the five-pounders to his neat grey quill.

As fry were hatching out with much success
  On Marston's fair preserve, we thought it fitting
With silver garniture his board to dress,
  That he might think of us while round it sitting—
The younglings wondering at its massiveness,
  His *cara sposa* sipping tea and knitting—
Nor deem we would his children's faith unsettle,
Although therewith we handed him the kettle.*

As Wilson in our service spent much time,
  What fitter than a watch, correct and golden,
With glittering chain enlink'd, like rhyme to rhyme,
  To mind him thro' the hours of memories olden?
The legend with simplicity sublime
  Recording how to him we felt beholden;
While both received (perhaps temptation risky!)
A silver flask for *eau de vie* or whisky.

---

* The story goes that three miners were seated round a copper
kettle outside a hovel in the North of England on a Sunday morning, when one of our Bishops on his way to a church to preach,
stopped and remarked how grieved he was to see them spending
their Sunday in that manner, and asked what they might be doing
with the kettle. "We're lying for it," said the miners. The
Bishop begged for an explanation. " The one of us as can tell
the biggest lie will get the kettle," said a spokesman, " your
worship can cut in if you like." " I ! " exclaimed the Bishop,
" why, I never told a lie in my life " " Lads," retorted the
miner, " hand him up the kettle ! "

The Founder rises 'mid our plaudits loud,
  And heartily, if hoarsely,* thanks the givers:
The Hon. Sec. follows, and declares how proud
  Such kindness made him! Then Sir Ford delivers
Deserved philippics 'gainst the boorish crowd
  Who here deplete and there pollute our rivers!
Then round the gifts that graced this famed house-
    warming,
All press and buzz, like honey bees when swarming.

Soon all disperse in groups for angling talk,
  And sips of Mocha, while above them curling,
Float rings that look like rises: then they walk
  In fancy by fair streams whose waters swirling
Chafe northern boulder, or soft southern chalk,
  And tell of takes of salmon, trout or herling;
Then join fraternal hands and shout in glee
One hearty, final " Floreat F. F. C.! "

---

  * Mr. Marston was suffering from so bad a cold that he was
hardly able to speak.

THE MARSTON MAYS.

On reading the poem, "An Invitation," sent by Professor John Duncan Quackenbos, of Columbia University, to Professor Trowbridge, of the same University, for a day's trout fishing on the Hammerasset, forwarded by their friend, Mr. A. Nelson Cheney, to the Editor of *The Fishing Gazette*, and published therein, June 18th, 1892, p. 417.

By thy window watching "the Marston Mays,"
    As they burst into tender green ;
While thy incense curls and fancy plays
    With the young Spring's golden sheen.
I see thee, Cheney, and feel thou art
A kindred spirit in mind and heart.

I, too, know well that joy of hope
    When the green doth tip the thorn ;
And the visions that come within thy scope,
    In the light of the glad May morn :
How they sing to thy soul of the flowing streams,
And fill it with brook and river dreams.

                                            M

That sap that stirs in " the Marston May "
   Is a sign of life that glows,
Where the Hammerasset's streamlets play
   By the banks where the alder grows,
And the fins of the trout are fanning to-day
With the life that throbs in " the Marston May."

You think of the day when the tender green
   Shall bloom into double red ;
And how it shall see you walk between,
   Rod-laden with joyous tread,
The form of dear Professor John,
And Trowbridge with his war-paint on.

Bosses of bloom will rose the green,
   And the green wear deeper shade ;
In ruddier spots, 'mid golden sheen,
   The trout will be arrayed ;
And then in the ear of leafy June
They will play on the reel a merry tune.

The flies in the sunbeam seem to sing
   To the music of the reel,
When the Mays and the Browns you long to fling,
   Shall help to fill your creel ;
And the rod shall bend in the graceful curve
That gladdens the heart and thrills the nerve.

But not of the sport of summer days
    Alone are you musing there ;
But of all that Nature's hand displays,
    In valley and woodland fair,
To the eyes that see and the heart that feels
The Love that loveliness reveals.

But "the Marston Mays " touch other springs
    In the angler's gentle soul,
And wakened Memory softly brings
    Unfolded, Friendship's scroll ;
And many a form appears to view
That hath wielded the rod in the past with you.

And some, like him who sent the May,
    You greet across "the Pond ";
And some, like the friends of this lovely lay,*
    Are dear by a closer bond ;
But friends unknown in our F. F. C.
Would claim a kind thought fraternally !

---

* See the poem referred to.

PROS AND CONS.

SOME affirm, For lively sport
    You may go to *sea*, sir:
I would say—I mean no ill—
    Rather go to *Dee*, sir;
Taste is all; let all who will
    Sojourn at the seaside,
I—excuse my *want* of taste—
    By far prefer the Deeside.

Some affirm, No fishing can
    Be e'er compared to bottom;
Others, and among them, I,
    The top's the place to pot 'em;
Yet when all is said and done,
    Your success the test is;
Whichever *you* can do the best,
    That for you the best is.

Some affirm, If goodly trout
    You at eve would dish up,
Never fish adown the stream,
    Rather always fish up:

I would say, Or up or down,
　As you freely wish, sir,
Guided by this rule alone,
　How can *you* catch fish, sir ?

Some affirm, Of woods for rods
　Best that stylèd lance is :
One man fancies hickory ;
　Bamboo, saith Francis Francis ;
For myself, I little care
　What the kind of wood is ;
If it suit my muscle well,
　Then I think it good is.

Some affirm, the rod for trout
　Should be one of ten feet ;*
Do they not in this forget
　That in fisher-*men*, feet
Differ as their muscles do,
　And as their length of bones, sir ?
And therefore what is long for Smith,
　Is far too short for Jones, sir.

Some advise, Play long your fish ;
　Others, Kill him quick, man !
As tho' all fish were game or tame,
　And all so long, so thick, man ;

---

* Notably W. C. Stewart in his " Practical Angler."

I judge by your fish, one fish
   Is no more like another
Than good and gentle Abel was
   Like Cain his wrathful brother.

Some affirm, Our English trout
   Have lately grown æsthetic ;
And that a green sou'-west of green.
   On Itchen is emetic :
Doubtless angling School Boards may
   Fishes' wits have whetted,
Yet I think, with shades of shades
   Trout need not be petted.

And when I read of salmon-flies
   In books of learnèd anglers,
And hear the jargon that is talk'd
   By colour-crazèd wranglers,
I often think, it is indeed
   Enough to make a pussy
Laugh in her sleep to dream that fish
   Can be one half so fussy.

I now dismiss you to your rod
   With my fraternal benison,
By borrowing this sage remark
   From laurell'd Alfred Tennyson,

" Others follies teach us not,
Nor much their wisdom teaches,
But most of sterling worth is what
Our own experience preaches."*

* Will Waterproof's Lyrical Monologue.

A LAY OF GOOD CHEER.

"The sport of the angler, 'tis clear as the day,
Needs patience above every other," they say;
And I fear there is truth in the adage; and why?
No sport has such trials that virtue to try!*

But take, brother angler, a cure for your care,
However things look, you need never despair;
Be never surprised when the hopeful day fails,
Nor hopeless when all that is adverse assails.

If the morning be such as to damp all your pluck,
At eve you may get quite a run of good luck:
If this pool, or that, yield you nought but despair,
The next may give treasure both ample and rare.

If your tackle give way, be your heart true and firm;
Let your spirit ne'er break like a poor, brittle worm;
Scour it well by true patience and render it tough;
Take the rough with the smooth, and 'twill hardly be
    rough.

* See, for example, " Dee-ceits and Dee-lusions," page 155.

If the wind's in the east, still of that make the best,
'Tis so fickle, it soon may chop round to the west ;
Nay, *fish* are so fickle, they sometimes will feast
When your hope is blown chill from the nor'ard of
    east.

If we find disappointment, yet spirits like ours
So tutor'd to patience, may laugh as it lours ;
We have always this solace to comfort our pain
That in seeking we find, and in losing we gain.

If the fish do not rise, still our sky doth not fall ;
We find " books in the running brooks," goodness in
    all ;
If we lose our hook'd fish, we find pastime and health,
And, tho' empty our creel be, in these we find wealth.

And whatever the trials with which we may cope,
We may always enjoy the sweet " pleasures of hope ; "
And good health and fresh air, and the music of
    streams,
Fill our days with pure pleasure, our nights with pure
    dreams.

VESPERS.

The sun doth set,
    And the moon doth rise,
And the shadows fall
    On tired eyes;
The mill-wheel stops,
    And the beetle's hum
Alone is heard
    In the woodland dumb.

The daisies close
    Their fringèd eyes,
Where the herd in the dew
    Of the meadow lies :
And Zephyr sighs,
    But holds his breath
As tho' he were awed
    By daylight's death.

A holy calm
  On the water broods,
And the stars creep out
  Of their solitudes,
While the lamb's last bleat
  From a distant pen
Is the cadence sweet
  Of a hymn's Amen.

MY APOLOGY FOR MY NAME.

BENEATH my breezy Saxon name,
I hide another—not for shame—
   Which, were it known, would rouse a ban
From narrow souls who cannot see
How one who sings of sport can be
   A merciful or Christian man.*

In spite of little minds like these,
So like the cynic Pharisees
   Who thought the Christ Himself no saint,†
I should not blush if my true name
Were on my page to rouse their blame,
   Nor should I feel it suffered taint.

I know some anglers would climb Hermon
As soon as sit to read a sermon,
   Or go to hear my censors preach ;
So I attempt in winsome ways
Such minds to higher things to raise
   By what their art itself can teach.

---

   * Matt. xvii. 27.   † Matt. xi. 19.

I write beneath a *nom de plume*
To give Fair Play a little room,
   And balk the shafts of Prejudice ;
For well I know the critic saith,
" What good can come from Nazareth ? "
   When "Nazareth " the author is.

So call me but a sporting man,
And place upon my book your ban ;
   That will not fill my heart with woe ;
Enough for me, my aim is high,
My motive pure, as *so* I try
   The halo round my sport to show.